MINE TO SAVE

JEN TALTY

JUPITER PRESS

This book is a work of fiction. Names, characters, places, and incidents are products of the author's imagination or used fictitiously. Any resemblance to actual events or locales or persons living or dead is entirely coincidental.

Copyright © 2022
by Jen Talty All rights reserved.

No part of this work may be used, stored, reproduced or transmitted without written permission from the publisher except for brief quotations for review purposes as permitted by law.
This book is licensed for your personal enjoyment only. This book may not be re-sold or given away to other people. If you would like to share this book with another person, please purchase an additional copy for each recipient. If you're reading this book and did not purchase it, or it was not purchased for your use only, please purchase your own copy.

MINE TO SAVE

A SAFE HARBOR NOVEL

USA Today Bestseller
JEN TALTY

PRAISE FOR JEN TALTY

"Deadly Secrets is the best of romance and suspense in one hot read!" *NYT Bestselling Author Jennifer Probst*

"A charming setting and a steamy couple heat up the pages in a suspenseful story I couldn't put down!" *NY Times and USA today Bestselling Author Donna Grant*

"Jen Talty's books will grab your attention and pull you into a world of relatable characters, strong personalities, humor, and believable storylines. You'll laugh, you'll cry, and you'll rush to get the next book she releases!" Natalie Ann USA Today Bestselling Author

"I positively loved *In Two Weeks*, and highly recommend it. The writing is wonderful, the story is fantastic, and the characters will keep you coming back for more. I can't wait to get my hands on future installments of the NYS Troopers series." *Long and Short Reviews*

"*In Two Weeks* hooks the reader from page one. This is a fast paced story where the development of the romance grabs you emotionally and the suspense keeps you sitting on the edge of your chair. Great characters, great writing, and a believable plot that can be a warning to all of us." *Desiree Holt, USA Today Bestseller*

"*Dark Water* delivers an engaging portrait of wounded hearts as the memorable characters take you on a healing journey of love. A mysterious death brings danger and intrigue into the drama, while sultry passions brew into a believable plot that melts the reader's heart. Jen Talty pens an entertaining romance that grips the heart as the colorful and dangerous story unfolds into a chilling ending." *Night Owl Reviews*

"This is not the typical love story, nor is it the typical mystery. The characters are well rounded and interesting." *You Gotta Read Reviews*

"*Murder in Paradise Bay* is a fast-paced romantic thriller with plenty of twists and turns to keep you guessing until the end. You won't want to miss this one..." *USA Today bestselling author Janice Maynard*

A NOTE FROM JEN TALTY

Welcome to Lighthouse Cove and the *SAFE HARBOR* series. This series will be all about finding our place in the world. Not just where we belong and who we belong with but searching for the one place we can feel at peace. A connection. Some people come to Lighthouse Cove to relax. To get away from the hustle and bustle of the outside world. However, everyone can agree they stay because the small seaside town gave them the safe harbor their souls craved and the love their hearts desired.

This is Emmett and Trinity's story. Trinity comes to Lighthouse Cove to speak with the last person who saw her father alive and to find answers. The last thing she expects is to find love. Grab a glass of vino, kick back, relax, and find safe harbor in this romantic story of finding true love when you least expect it.

BOOK DESCRIPTION

Trinity Hughes has spent a lifetime resenting her biological father. However, now that he's dead, Trinity wants to set the record straight. Her father might have killed one man thirty-five years ago, but he paid his debt to society. She knows deep in her soul that he did not murder sixteen men in South Florida and she's going to prove it. All she needs is a little help from the last man who saw her father alive.

After ending a six-year relationship, Local police officer Emmett Kirby has given up on love and family, dedicating himself to a career that has been the cornerstone of his life. And he's happy to do it. The citizens of Lighthouse Cove have always come first. However, when a stranger comes through town and is accused of murder, and then killed right in front of him, Emmett questions the investigation and what he uncovers he not only doesn't like, but it puts himself, and Trinity in the center of a twisted plan that could make them a killers next victim.

1

*E*mmett Kirby stepped into the Safe Harbor Cafe and inhaled sharply. The rich scent of bitter coffee mixed with sugar, cinnamon, maple syrup, and butter melting over a big piece of egg-coated sourdough bread assaulted his nostrils. He'd been looking forward to this meal since his eyes blinked open at four this morning.

"Look what the cat dragged in." Lucy Ann stepped from around the hostess station and gave him a big hug. "I haven't seen you in here for a few days. I started to wonder if you'd found a better place to grab a bite."

"Never." He laughed. "Besides, imagine what Phil would do to me if I did. You'd never find my body."

She looked him up and down. "This coming from

the one carrying the gun." She squeezed his biceps. "There's a free booth in the back. Go have a seat. I'll get your order started."

"Phil's not here?"

"Opal's got some weird stomach bug, so she stayed home from school today. It's his turn to have kid duty."

"Poor Opal. She's not an easy one to keep down." Emmett scanned the diner, making a note of everyone and everything, more out of habit than anything else. His mother, the chief of police, had drilled it into his head to make sure he knew every detail of every room. It was both a blessing and a curse.

"Trust me, I know. I love that kid, but I'd rather be here working than trying to get her to rest." Lucy Ann shook her head and let out a long breath. "This morning, she came running into our room. I mean, she'd been throwing up all night, yet there she was, barreling at us, babbling about something. Then, all of a sudden, she stopped talking and got sick right there. Didn't even try to make it to a toilet."

Emmitt covered his mouth to stifle a laugh. He shouldn't find any of that funny, but he did, especially because he knew Opal. That girl was why children should be made with an off button.

"You wait. Someday, you'll have children."

His heart hit his gut like a sinking ship. "I'm too old for that."

"You're forty. You're not too old to find love again and have kids." Lucy Ann gave him that all-knowing look that made his insides twist.

He knew she meant well, and her intensions were good. But Emmett wasn't about to have this conversation. Especially with Lucy Ann. He loved her like a sister, but other than his ex-fiancée, Melinda, he didn't discuss having children, and even then, he preferred to sweep it under the rug. It wasn't anyone's business. Besides, he'd done everything he could to accept it. That was all that mattered.

He glanced at his watch. "I've only got about half an hour before I need to get back out there and keep our little town safe."

Lucy Ann wrapped her arms around her middle. "I heard there was a murder less than fifty miles south of us yesterday. That makes sixteen men killed in just two years."

"It does." Emmett saw no reason to lie to anyone about those facts. There was a state-wide manhunt on for a suspect.

A one, Jeff Allen. Sixty-seven-year-old known

felon. He'd murdered his wife's lover thirty-five years ago. He'd been out of jail for twenty-seven and off the radar for the last twenty.

"But you have nothing to worry about." He squeezed her forearm in hopes of reassuring her. The entire town had been on edge as each murder got a little closer to home. "Phil doesn't fit the victimology."

"You really believe this guy is only killing cheaters?"

"That's what the feds believe, and he's been leaving behind notes that indicate that, so…yes. I do. Don't worry. Okay?"

She nodded. "I'll get your coffee."

"Thanks." He strolled to the back of the diner and took a seat, making sure his back was to the wall.

It was late in the morning, so the breakfast crowd had dwindled to a few stragglers finishing their second cups of coffee while either avoiding whatever they needed to do that day, or simply not wanting to go out into the world just yet—something he could relate to.

One of the waitresses brought over a large cup of black brew.

He sat in his booth and sipped his hot beverage, squinting as an older gentleman with a long, scraggly beard and stained clothing entered the diner. Emmett knew every homeless person who lived in his small town, and this man was new.

Emmett pushed his mug to the side and sat up a little taller.

Of course, someone new strolled through their peaceful safe harbor as they made their way south for the winter or north for the summer every year. The homeless were no different than all the snowbirds who came to this part of Florida.

This man was tall and thin. Too thin. He looked as if he hadn't eaten in days. His eyes were sunken, and his skin discolored. Almost yellow.

He looked around nervously and pulled his coat —which he didn't need since it was close to eighty outside—tight across his body.

That wasn't necessarily something that gave Emmett pause or reason for concern, but when the stranger noticed Emmett and locked gazes with him, *that* did.

To make matters worse, the man glanced over his shoulder. Not once. Not twice. But three times.

Emmett understood that cops made a lot of people nervous. But this guy wasn't just jittery. He looked downright terrified. The man glanced around the diner.

Emmett rested his hand on his weapon.

The man looked familiar. Emmett knew he'd seen him somewhere, only it hadn't been in Lighthouse Cove.

Where, then?

He searched the files in his brain, but he couldn't place the face.

The man inched closer, keeping his focus on Emmett and nowhere else. "Do you have a minute?" the man asked as he stood at the end of the booth.

"Sure," Emmett said. His job was to protect and serve all citizens. This man was no exception.

"May I sit down?"

Emmett nodded.

"I apologize for interrupting. I won't take up too much of your time." The man scratched the side of his face as he eased onto the bench, barely sitting on the edge. His beard was long and tangled, his hair much the same. He smelled like five-day-old cheese left out in the elements.

"What can I help you with?" Emmett asked.

"I was hoping you could get a message to someone." The man glanced over his shoulder.

"Who?"

"My daughter."

"What's her name?" Emmett took his hand off his

pistol and rested both on the table as a sign that he wasn't threatened in any way. However, something about this man worried Emmett.

"Everything is in this envelope." The man took out a legal-sized package from inside his coat. "You can open it once they've taken me away."

"Once who has taken you away?" Emmett's pulse kicked up a notch. He kept his hands flattened on the table, but he was ready for anything.

"It doesn't matter. I just need to know that when this is over, you're going to give this to my daughter."

"I need to know your name and hers if I'm going to do that." He needed to know a lot more about this guy and what the hell was going on, but he'd start there.

His radio crackled in his ear. "Emmett. Where are you?" His mother's voice came over the radio. "We're about to have a situation at the diner. State, feds, and SWAT are rolling in."

Shit. He blinked. It all came together like a kaleidoscope in his brain. The images pinned to the board at the station flashed in his mind.

Jeff Allen.
Serial killer.

Emmett tapped the mic on his shoulder. "I'm at the diner right now," he said. "Having breakfast."

"They aren't going to let me walk out of here alive." Jeff pushed the envelope across the table. "Please. Make sure she gets it. My legacy depends on it." He stood.

"What the hell do you think you're doing?" Emmett jumped to his feet.

Tears rolled down Jeff's cheeks and into his facial hair. "I didn't do it. I've killed only one man in my life, and I served my time in prison for it. I didn't murder anyone else. Tell my daughter that. Make her believe it." Jeff took a step back and pulled out a gun. He waved it around like a wild animal. "No one is leaving," he said. "Give me your weapon or I'll start shooting."

"If you fire that pistol, I won't be able to tell your daughter anything." Carefully, Emmett unholstered his service revolver and handed it to Jeff as he continued to assess the situation.

A mother and her two small children huddled in the front booth while a young couple snuggled together at the counter.

Lucy Ann stood stoically at the hostess station, and the cooks emerged from the back room.

All in all, there were ten people in the diner, including Jeff and Emmett.

A SWAT van rolled into the parking lot, along with a couple of federal and state vehicles and his mother's patrol car.

Of all the people out there, his mom was the only one he trusted completely.

"I didn't want it to end this way, but that agent out there didn't leave me any choice."

Emmett had no idea what this man was talking about, but he didn't want this to turn into a blood bath. He pressed the mic on his shoulder. "Tell them to stand down. I'm chatting with the suspect now."

Jeff pointed his gun toward Lucy Ann.

Emmett inched closer to the door, stepping between Jeff and his friend. "Why don't we sit back down, and you can tell me what you know?"

"Someone is setting me up. I didn't do anything wrong. I would never hurt anyone."

"You went to prison for murder. You killed your wife's lover. You never denied murdering him," Emmett said.

"I paid my debt to society for that. Since then, the worst I've done is taken food from dumpsters to survive."

"You're pointing a gun at a woman who's done nothing to you. That's pretty bad."

"I don't want to hurt anyone. I only want my daughter to get what's in that envelope."

"Why don't you let all these innocent people go, and you and I can talk this out?"

"No." Jeff shook his head like a wild dog. "If I do that, they will come rushing through that door and take me into custody. I won't stand a chance. They won't listen to me."

Emmett glanced out the window. "Do you see that woman wearing a uniform just like mine, talking with one of the federal agents?"

"Yes," Jeff said.

"That's my boss. The one you heard on the radio. She can help negotiate, but you've got to be willing to give them something."

Jeff continued aiming his weapon at Lucy Ann, which annoyed the fuck out of Emmett. Not that he wanted it pointed at anyone else in the room. "How do you see this ending?" Emmett asked.

Jeff laughed. "We both know it's not going to end with me walking out of here at this point."

"It doesn't have to be that way."

"I'm tired," Jeff said. "My daughter hasn't wanted to talk to me since I was released from prison. I can't say as I blame her. But I tried to be a good man. I tried to play by society's rules. Do you know how hard it is to get a second chance once you fuck up as badly as I did?"

"I can't imagine," Emmett said.

"Everyone says that if they ever caught their spouse cheating, they'd do something drastic like kill someone. But the second they hear I actually saw red and did it, they change their tune."

Flashes of Emmett's childhood came flooding into his brain. His mother's affair had torn their family apart. All the fighting. All the times his father had stormed out of the house.

Not to mention what it had done to his brother when he'd found out that his father wasn't his biological dad.

However, no one had resorted to murder.

"I lost my family and my job. I spent eight years in prison. Seven more on probation. Do you know how hard it is to find a job as a convicted felon? No matter what I did. No matter how many times I apologized, I couldn't get anyone to trust me. Not even when I moved from one town to the next. All I wanted was a fresh start and a chance to have a relationship with my daughter. But she wouldn't have anything to do with me. She believes I'm a monster, and now I'm sure that point is being driven home. But it's not true." Jeff shook his head. "The only person I have ever killed was Paul, and I honestly didn't mean to do that."

The radio crackled in Emmett's ear. "What's going on in there, Emmett?" his mother asked.

"Jeff. You need to let me talk to them out there." He tapped his mic and glanced to his right. A couple of federal agents were talking with his mom while the SWAT team waited for instructions. He let go of the radio button. "How about if I step outside and buy you some time?"

"Time for what?"

"To tell your story. Tell me why we should believe you."

"You can't leave the diner," Jeff said.

"Can I use my cell?"

Jeff nodded.

Slowly, Emmett reached into his pocket. He carefully lifted out his phone and tapped his mom's contact information. She answered on the second ring.

"You okay?" his mother asked.

"Yup."

"We've got to get those people out of there."

"I know," Emmett said. "He has an envelope he wants me to make sure his daughter gets."

"We can do that," his mother said. "What other demands does he have?"

"None right now. Hang on." He dropped his cell to his side. "I want to hear what you have to say, and they will give us some time to talk, but you've got to let some of these people go. If you don't, this is going to get ugly real fast."

Jeff nodded. "All the women and children can go."

"I'm sending out some hostages now," Emmett said into the phone. "Jeff's going to tell me why we should believe he's innocent. I need time. You need to make sure that happens."

"I'm not going to let these yahoos storm in while my son's the one doing the negotiating. But don't let this go on too long. Got it?"

"Yes, ma'am." He tapped the screen. "Listen. I'm going to be straight with you, Jeff. My boss out there happens to be my mom, and we work a little differently than the feds. So, I want you to take a step back. If you're in the line of fire, they might try to take you out. I'll open the door and let the hostages go."

Jeff let out a long breath. "I never wanted it to come to this," he said. "I wanted to get that information to my daughter and be done with it." He sat on one of the stools at the counter, still holding the gun, pointing it at one of the cooks, who stood paralyzed by the kitchen door.

Emmett held open the front door, and all the women and children raced out. The rest, minus the cook, huddled in the far corner of the diner.

Quickly, Emmett snagged the envelope off the table and placed it on the counter before pouring two cups of coffee. "So, tell me, Jeff. Why should we believe you didn't murder sixteen men? Because based on the note that was left at all the scenes, it all points back to you."

Jeff lifted the mug with a shaky hand and took a sip of the hot liquid. He didn't bother to blow into it or anything. "I'm being set up. I don't know why. Or by who. But I saw a man following me. Not another homeless man either."

"How do you know he was following you?"

"Because I saw him in Miami. Fort Lauderdale. Again in Delray. And I saw him yesterday down in West Palm." Jeff lifted his gaze. "If someone is cheating, I wouldn't be surprised if you have a dead body on your hands shortly."

Someone was always cheating—sad, but true.

"I'm not accusing you." Emmett held up his hands. "But that sounds like you know something."

"No. But I know there have been five deaths in the last six months. They follow me wherever I go, and some note about Paul and meeting him in Hell is always left at the crime scene."

It had been stupid for the police to release that to the press. But it wasn't Emmett's case. At least, not until now.

"When did you find out about the killings?"

"Every couple of weeks, I try to stay at a homeless shelter to get a shower, a change of clothes, and a good meal. That kind of thing. Also, to watch the news and see what's going on in the world. That's when I found out that I was a wanted man."

"How long ago?" Emmett asked more specifically.

"A year," Jeff said. "I've since learned there have been sixteen murders. All in cities I've lived in. But I didn't do it. I swear to God. It wasn't me. But I can't prove it. The only thing I have is in that envelope. There's a sketch of the man I saw following me. Also dates and times of where I saw him."

"Have you seen him here in Lighthouse Cove?"

"No, sir," Jeff said. "But that doesn't mean he's not here."

"Why did you want your daughter to have that and not the police?"

"I knew you'd look at the contents, but I want my daughter to know I'm innocent. That I didn't do what I'm being accused of." Jeff pushed the coffee mug aside and stood. "My life has been over for a long time. My daughter has had to live most of her life knowing her father killed her mother's lover in a fit of rage. I might not have meant to do it, but I did. I owned up to my mistake and I did my time. But this? I didn't do it. However, no one is going to believe me." He let out a dry laugh.

"I can tell you're a good man with a kind soul, but even you are struggling to believe me, and I guess I can't blame you. Like I said. I'm tired. I can't go on like this anymore." Jeff pointed at the envelope. "Make sure my daughter gets that, and if you get a chance to talk to her, tell her that a day never went by that I didn't think about her." He gripped the gun.

"What are you doing?" Emmett's pulse increased.

"It's over for me." He held his weapon in the general direction of a few people huddled in the corner as he made his way toward the door.

A red light filtered through the glass.

Shit. That wasn't a good sign. "Jeff, step away from the front of the diner."

"It doesn't matter anymore," Jeff said. "The feds are going to kill me, and if they don't, I'll get murdered on the inside. My life is over. I know it. But I don't want my daughter to have to live with this legacy, too. I've documented where I've been since the murders started to the best of my ability. The jobs I've had. The places I've stayed. It's all there. Hopefully, you can help my girl so she doesn't have to live with this again." He gave Emmett an odd smile. "This is a really nice little town you have. It's like a tiny safe harbor."

"I would have to agree with that statement," Emmett said. "Why don't you let it be yours?"

"That ship has sailed for me, but maybe you can help it be that for my daughter," Jeff said. "Make sure she gets the information in that envelope. Tell her I didn't do it and ask her to help clear my name. Can you do that for me?"

"I can, but why don't you do it with me?" Emmett said. "Jeff, let me talk with the feds. I'll make sure you're heard."

"I appreciate that." Jeff opened the door and took two steps outside. He raised the pistol in an aggressive move toward the police.

Pop. Pop.

"Fuck." Emmett raced across the diner and out

the front door to Jeff's side. "Why the hell did you do that?" He kicked the weapon, making sure there was no way Jeff could reach it—not that he would since Emmett was pretty sure he was dead. He reached down and pressed his fingers against Jeff's neck.

Yup.

Dead.

"Shit," Emmett mumbled as he looked up. "That wasn't necessary."

His mother ran up the stairs.

Some federal agent yelled at her to stand down.

She turned around and flipped him off, uttering a few curse words under her breath. "You okay?"

"Yes. Except I'm pissed off. He didn't need to die."

"Agreed."

State police and federal agents stormed the building.

"Hang on." Emmett made his way back inside as quickly as he could and found the envelope.

"What is that?"

"He told me he was being set up and that someone was following him." Emmett glanced around, ensuring the other cops were doing something else as he checked the contents.

A couple of sketches.

A ledger of dates, times, and places. It didn't make sense. Yet.

And a note to a woman by the name of Trinity Hughes with some contact information.

Emmett took pictures of everything before stuffing it all back into the envelope. He knew damn well that he and his mother's little local police department would be cut out of the loop about as fast as the feds had taken that kill shot.

He still couldn't believe they'd done that so quickly. They didn't even give Jeff a warning. Granted, the man had a loaded weapon pointed in their direction…

"Do you believe him?" his mother asked.

"I don't know," Emmett admitted. "There was something about him that makes me want to look into his story a little more closely."

"If there are no more murders, they're going to believe they got their man. And to be honest, that will make sense."

"Unless he was right, and he's being set up."

"But why would someone do that?"

Emmett had no idea, but he intended to find out, and he thought he'd start with contacting the daughter.

2

Trinity ignored the half-dozen text messages from her friend Kathy at the yoga studio, along with a few other friends.

They all wanted to know the same thing. While the answer appeared obvious, it wasn't.

She sat on the edge of the sofa in her mother's family room, gripping her mom's hand. A picture of her biological father flashed across the screen. She barely recognized him, and if she were being honest, she wasn't sure she could have picked him out of a lineup even if he hadn't grown an eight-inch beard and had hair down past his shoulders.

She didn't remember her father. Not really, anyway. She'd been told he'd died shortly after her first birthday. All she had of him were photographs, and even those were few and far between.

But the truth was, her father had gone to prison for manslaughter. There had been no trial. He'd pled guilty to the charges, and the judge had sentenced him to the maximum under penalty of law. He served eight of those fifteen years in prison, and then seven living in a halfway house while on parole.

When he finished out his sentence and left Pensacola, Florida for good, she'd only been sixteen. But before he left, he'd reached out to her. She'd wanted to see him, so had agreed to meet with him. By then, she knew that he wasn't dead thanks to an article that'd come out revealing all the dirty little details.

But that had been the last time she'd seen or spoken to her father, and she'd had some harsh words for him that day.

She'd been a teenager with an enormous chip on her shoulder. One who had just learned that all the adults in her life were liars, and that her biological father wasn't dead, after all.

Nope. He'd been in prison and then on parole because he had a wicked temper and had beaten a man to death with his bare hands. She'd wanted to see what kind of man could do that with his child sleeping in the other room.

Of course, she had anger and resentment toward her mother, as well. The worst had been hearing about how her mom had been screwing some other guy, and how her husband had walked in on them and then went ballistic.

In a way, Trinity almost couldn't blame her dad.

But he'd killed a man. There was no excuse for it. And on the day she'd met her father, she'd told him that she wished he'd died for real.

Now, he was legit dead.

She'd said those same words to her mom and Ben, but she'd had time and space to heal those wounds and had taken it back.

She hadn't gotten that chance with her biological father, and she'd wanted to change that. A few years ago, she'd hired a private investigator to find him, but when the PI found her dad, she could bring herself to contact him.

And now she'd never be able to say what she needed.

She glanced in her mother's direction. "There's no way he could have done what the police are saying, is there?"

Her mom swiped at her cheeks. "Your father was a lot of things, but a serial killer? I don't think so."

"I have to agree with you, Mother," Ben, the man Trinity had called *Father* since the age of five, said as he handed her a cup of hot tea. "I spoke with your dad the week he left town. He was bitter. Angry, even. But at himself. No one else. Well, maybe your mother for her actions and for letting you believe he was dead."

Trinity had forgiven her mother long ago. However, twinges of that anger bubbled to the surface. While she understood that her mom had thought her lie would protect Trinity, the reality was that she was simply hiding the shame of her affair and what it had done to their family. She hadn't wanted her only daughter to know that perhaps she'd had a hand in what'd happened.

Well, no matter what her mother had done, Paul Lewis hadn't deserved to be murdered by her father.

But her dad hadn't killed sixteen other men. Trinity felt that certainty deep to her core.

"No. Your father wasn't a murderer. Not the way they are saying," her mother said softly. "At least, not the man I knew."

"He tried to contact me." Trinity hadn't known

what to do a few months ago when a random call had come in from a social worker at a homeless shelter in South Florida. But by the time she'd gotten the nerve to call back, her father had left. Trinity had left her contact information, but her dad never called again.

"Are you serious? Why didn't you say anything?" Ben asked.

She shrugged. "I figured you'd both try to talk me out of calling him back. And, honestly, I wasn't sure I was going to. But it was too late anyway. He'd already moved on." That had been the second opportunity she'd had in her adult life to reconnect with her biological father.

"Oh, sweetheart," her mother said. "I'm sorry."

"Where is Lighthouse Cove?" Trinity asked.

"It's about a half hour north of West Palm Beach," Ben said. "Why? You're not thinking of going there, are you?"

"I want to find out what happened."

"It's all over the news." Her mother leaned over, lifted her glass of wine off the coffee table, and took a big swig. "I'm not sure there's much else to find out."

"They can't just say that he's guilty and be done with it," Trinity said.

"Of course, not." Ben sat next to her and took her

hand. "I don't know much about police procedure, but I'm sure they need to gather proof and collect evidence before they can close the case."

She pointed at the television. "That federal agent, Jenna Robash, has pretty much called my father a serial killer. She ended her press conference with something to the effect of: *The citizens of South Florida can sleep easy now that we've caught the Adultery Killer.* I'd say that means they are washing their hands of this."

"I don't want to believe this, but maybe something happened to your father. He's been living on the streets for so long," her mom said. "Maybe he's been doing drugs and lost his mind."

Trinity sucked in a deep breath and then let it out slowly, counting to ten. Sure, she could understand why anyone, including her mother—no, *especially* her mother—would say something like that, but it didn't mean it was true. Far from it. "Dad never took drugs."

"We don't know him at all anymore." Ben squeezed her hand. "I don't want to believe he would do something so terrible. The few times I spoke to him while he was in prison and during his probation, all I saw was a broken man who lived with a ton of remorse. But that kind of guilt can change a person. Both prison and being homeless can harden a man."

Deep down, Trinity knew that Ben was right. And what did she know anyway? She didn't know a single thing about him, so she couldn't make even the tiniest judgment—neither good nor bad. "I don't mean to bring this up, Mom, but I wish you had told me the truth."

"What truth? Because if I had told you that your biological father was in prison, I would have had to tell you why and that wasn't something I was prepared to tell my daughter."

Trinity held up her hand. "Keeping that from me destroyed any chance I had of having any kind of relationship with him."

"Your mother didn't want you to have one. And, to be honest, neither did I," Ben said. "At least not while you were a child. As an adult, you were free to make that choice. But not at sixteen."

This wasn't the first time they'd had this argument, and it probably wouldn't be the last. But at least they'd stopped yelling. Trinity could understand why Ben and her mom had done it. If she were honest with herself, if she'd had a kid, she might have done the exact same thing.

"Just because your dad was remorseful for what

he did doesn't change the fact that he killed Paul—right in front of your mother, with you sleeping in the room next door."

Trinity wanted to add that her mother and Paul had been doing something they shouldn't have been doing while she was sleeping in the room next door, but she refrained. There was no point in hurting her mother by bringing that tidbit up. What was done was done. However, there was one thing she would never let go. "You should have let me see him," she said. "It could have been supervised. But he was my father, and by taking any contact with him away from me, you changed how I saw him."

"We did what we thought was best for you at the time." Ben would never change his stance, and why would he? It was his truth. And her mother's.

"I know," Trinity said. "And knowing who I was back then, I might not have wanted to see him, but I can't help but wonder if all this would have played out differently if we'd all made different choices."

"I'm sorry, sweetheart, but your father killed a man." Her mother's expression turned hard. "Yes. I know. I was cheating, and I don't make excuses for my behavior. But that doesn't give anyone permission to murder another person." Her mother swiped a finger across her cheek.

Trinity's cell phone rang. She glanced at the screen.

"Lighthouse Cove Police Department?" she said softly. She tapped the green button. "Hello?"

"Is this Trinity Hughes?"

She took her tea and stood, heading to the den. "Yes. Who is this, please?"

"My name is Lieutenant Emmett Kirby with the Lighthouse Cove Police Department."

"I saw you on the news. You were with my father when they shot him." She swallowed the bitter taste that had bubbled up to her throat. "Why did they shoot him? Was he threatening people?"

"Ma'am. I'd like to speak with you if possible. In person, if that's okay with you. I can be in Pensacola tomorrow afternoon."

"No. I'll come to you."

"It's not necessary for you to make the trip. Besides, I'm sure the FBI and the state police will be calling. This is their case. To be honest, I'm asking to speak with you unofficially."

"Why?" She pinched the bridge of her nose. "If you're not trying to close a bunch of murder cases and make a name for yourself, or tracking down other leads because maybe my father didn't kill all those men, then why do you want to talk with me?"

Hell, why did anyone want to have a conversation with her? She knew nothing about her father.

"I spoke with your dad before he died. He gave me an envelope, which is now with the FBI, but he wanted you to have it. I took pictures of the contents and thought maybe you'd want to see them. Perhaps it could shed some light on some of the things he said to me."

"Wait. I'm confused. If the feds have the envelope, and my dad wanted me to have it, why aren't they banging on my door?"

"I don't have an answer for that, and while I told them what he told me, it's evidence. Though I'm not sure how they will use it. Anyway, I sure would like to sit down and speak with you, if that's okay."

"Like I said, I'll come to you. I'd like to see where my father died and retrace his last few days." She took a seat in the oversized chair in her mother's den. As a little girl, she'd always loved snuggling next to her mom in this very chair while she read her a bedtime story.

"Are you really sure you want to do that? No offense, but people in this town might not be too receptive, considering what they're accusing him of —and I mean no disrespect by that, ma'am."

Right. She doubted that, especially since she was

talking to a cop. His job was to believe that her father was guilty. "None taken," she lied. "I have a different last name. That should help."

"It should."

"Then it's settled."

"Okay. I'll text you an address where we can meet since this an unofficial visit, and all my contact information. Just let me know when you're in town," Emmett said. "Do you need a recommendation for a hotel? Because if you do, there's a great little bed and breakfast right on the water in town, and I can make sure you have a room."

"That would be amazing, thank you."

"I'll set it up. See you sometime tomorrow."

The phone went silent.

She dropped her head back and closed her eyes. She had no idea what to expect when she met with Emmett Kirby. A list of questions had already formed in her mind. There were things she wanted to know about her father, but she doubted this Emmett fella could answer them all. However, maybe he could point her in the right direction to find those answers.

Tap. Tap.

"Hey, sweetheart," her mother whispered. "Are you okay?"

"I am." Trinity nodded. "I'm going to head to South Florida tomorrow morning for a few days. Maybe a week."

"Why would you do that?" Her mom leaned against the doorjamb with a full wine glass in her hand. "It doesn't make any sense."

"I want to speak to the people who last spoke to my father. I want to somehow find a way to feel connected to him," she admitted.

"I know you. You're going to try to prove that he didn't murder those men, and I'm telling you, that is a mistake."

"What is? Trying to prove he didn't do it? Or believing it?" The words came out a little harsher than Trinity had planned. The last thing she wanted to do was hurt her mother.

"That's not fair. I've told you, I struggle to believe Jeff could have done the horrible things he's accused of. But he changed after my affair. After he killed Paul." Her mom took a big gulp of her beverage. "He changed before I started sleeping with Paul. I know this is no excuse, but I married your father because I was pregnant with you. I don't regret that decision because having you was the best thing that has ever happened to me. But I didn't love him the way he loved me. I know that's not fair to you or your dad, but it's the truth, and if I had been honest from the beginning, maybe *none* of this would have happened. That's something I've had to live with since Paul died."

"Mom, his death wasn't your fault." Trinity pushed to her feet and embraced her mother. "I'm sorry if I made you think that's how I felt."

"No. It's not you. It's me." Her mother palmed Trinity's cheek. "Most days, I can reconcile that your father's actions were his and his alone. However, there are moments where I rewind to what Paul and I were doing, and I know the buck stops there. I made a choice not to tell you about your dad because I thought I could spare you the pain of what happened."

"You must have known that someone would tell me some day."

"Your name was different, and we moved one town over. I honestly didn't think anyone would put it together. However, once your father finished his sentence, and that reporter decided to do that exposé exposing our dirty little secret, you became so angry at the world. I didn't think it would be healthy for you to see him, and I don't think it's a good idea for you to go chasing down a ghost now."

"I'm not sixteen anymore," Trinity said.

"Maybe not. But you have to know the reason I didn't want you to see your father after you found everything out. It was because of the things you were going through—all that anger and your temper. I was worried about you and how you'd respond once you met him."

"You think I'm going to revert back to being an angry adolescent?"

"I didn't say that. However, I don't think you should go digging into whatever it is your father has been doing for the last twenty years. What if you don't like what you find?"

"I need to know, Mom. Or at least I need to try to fill in some holes. Can you understand and support me on that?"

"Of course, I can. But do you have to go tomorrow?"

Trinity laughed. "If I don't, you'll keep trying to talk me out of it."

"What about work?"

"I've already got the next few shifts in the emergency room covered, and I'm going to call my supervisor at the hospital right now. I've got a ton of days saved up, and I haven't taken a single vacation or sick day in over two months. Don't worry. I'm not going to let anything interfere with my career as a nurse. I've worked too hard to get where I am."

Her mom let out an exasperated sigh. "Promise me you won't become obsessed with this."

"I'll do my best. Now, I'd better get home and pack. I've got a long drive ahead of me." She waited until her mother was out of the room before pulling up Kathy's contact information. She might as well get that phone call out of the way.

"Oh, my God. Are you okay?" Kathy asked. "I can't believe they shot him. Dead."

"Well, hello to you, too," Trinity mumbled.

"Sorry. But I can't believe it. He must have done something in that diner or threatened someone."

Trinity pinched the bridge of her nose. "He didn't kill those men. It doesn't make any sense."

"Oh, honey. I know you want to believe that, but—"

"I'm headed to Lighthouse Cove tomorrow. I'm going to meet with a police officer there who saw the whole thing."

"Why would you do that?" Kathy meant well, just like everyone else in Trinity's life. But they all wanted to think the worst of her biological father. And she understood that because she'd done that same thing for years.

But not anymore. It was time to get all the facts before making any judgments.

"Because I have questions that need answers."

"I'll come with you," Kathy said. "You shouldn't do this alone. This is when you need your friends the most. And what if this cop isn't who he says he is?"

Trinity didn't need a lecture. She needed support. But she sure as shit didn't need a babysitter. "No. This is something I need to do alone."

"Well, promise me you'll stay in touch. I can find someone to take over my yoga classes and be there in a snap. All you have to do is call. Okay?"

"Thanks, Kathy. I appreciate it." Trinity ended the call. She blew out a puff of air. If her father *did* do the things he'd been accused of, Trinity didn't know how she would survive the emotions that already churned her gut.

3

"You want me to do what?"

"You heard me." Emmett stared at his ex-fiancée and smiled. It was rare that Emmett asked his ex for much, even though they had a decent relationship. It had taken them a while to get to this point, and if anyone in Lighthouse Cove would understand Trinity's situation, it would be Melinda—only Emmett wasn't going to tell her, which made this tricky.

"You're lucky I even have anything. Who is this woman to you anyway?" Melinda asked as she fluffed one of the pillows that belonged to the lounge chairs by the pool. This house had one of the best views on the inlet. It had been in Melinda's family for three generations, and her mother had turned it into a bed and breakfast after Melinda's father went to prison.

It felt weird to be back at the bed and breakfast. It had fourteen bedrooms, sixteen bathrooms, and two state-of-the-art kitchens. The southern beach décor was impeccable, and there was always a waitlist to get a room in season.

"No one." That was the truth. "I don't even know her."

"Then why am I comping her room for as long as she needs it if you're not involved with her?"

Emmett contemplated telling Melinda right off the bat who Trinity was and why she needed the room. Melinda was one of the smartest people he knew, and she'd likely figure it out eventually. Of course, Melinda probably wouldn't be too bothered by it. But her guests might be. So, if he told her, she might say no to Trinity staying at the B&B.

Better to ask for forgiveness later.

"Because I'm asking you as a favor."

"You're fucking her, aren't you? If you are, it's about damn time you got yourself a girlfriend."

He laughed. "If that were the case, she'd be staying at my house and not here with you, because that would be weird."

"This place has a view. Your place, not so much."

She waved her hand across the deck toward the inlet that let out to the ocean. A large boat cruised by as it made its way toward the open water. "I can see you wanting to impress a lady at the same time flaunting a new relationship in my face." She stuck her nose in the air and tried not to smile, but her teasing tone wasn't lost on Emmett. It was nice that they had been able to put their painful breakup in the past. He would always have a special place in his heart for Melinda, and at the end of the day, all he wanted was for her to be happy.

"What's to flaunt when you have Chad?"

"Chad's away on business for the next week," she said with a pouty face.

"He's traveling a lot again?"

"I know that traveling comes with his job, and that's never going to change. I have to accept it because he loves what he does. It makes him happy."

Two things had driven a wedge between Melinda and Emmett.

The first one had been his job as a police officer. There were so many things she hated about it. It was dangerous. Stressful. He worked with his family. The hours.

She hadn't liked anything about his career.

It was why she and his brother's ex-wife used to

get along so well. However, she had supported him and never asked him to quit. She just complained. It was nice to see she'd stopped doing that with Chad.

It just showed that, in the end, they really weren't as perfect for each other as they thought they were.

And then there was the baby thing. The second Melinda had found out that Emmett couldn't give her a child of her own, she was out the door. Okay, it hadn't been that fast, but she wanted a child, and adoption wasn't even on the table. Though that wasn't entirely true either.

But that was the direction Emmett would have preferred to go in.

Too many children needed to be loved.

He and Melinda couldn't see eye to eye on the subject, and they had drifted apart. Or maybe they'd both checked out. Her biological clock was ticking, and Emmett had been feeling a tad sorry for himself.

And, at the end of the day, and with how quickly she and Chad had fallen in love, Emmett knew they'd made the right decision by breaking up.

"I mean, we're trying to get pregnant, and his trips are making that impossible in one way. But it's making it possible financially, so it's all a catch twenty-two."

"Too much information, Melinda," Emmett said,

but there it was, the reason for the extra crankiness. Melinda wanted a baby, and she wanted it yesterday. "But since you brought it up, and I'm not the man in your life, I'm going to say something to you."

"I don't need a lecture."

"This isn't a lecture," he said softly. "Do you love him?"

"I married him. Of course, I do."

"I know how important the baby thing is to you, so you need to remember what the doctor said."

"Yeah. Yeah. The more I stress, the less likely it is to happen." She blew out a puff of air. "I'm trying to relax. Really. I am." She squared her shoulders and smiled.

He chuckled. "So, can Trinity have a room or not?"

"One hundred bucks a week. That will cover the cost of food and whatnot."

"I think that's fair." Emmett dug his hand into his pocket. "I'll give cash now for a week. If we need it longer, I'll give you more."

"I appreciate it." She curled her fingers around his biceps. "I saw the news. I can't believe what happened. Someone could have gotten killed."

Now that Emmett had had time to process everything, he honestly didn't believe he'd been in any real danger. But he couldn't tell anyone that. "No one did."

"No one was injured thanks to you—except that murderer." Melinda had always praised Emmett, though she'd done it privately. "Lucy Ann said it was terrifying but that you were calm and knew exactly how to handle things."

"It's my job." Emmett's smartwatch vibrated. He glanced at the screen. "She's five minutes away."

Melinda tilted her head and puckered her lips. "Are you going to stand there and tell me that you told her I'd comp her room?"

"No. I told her I'd get her a room here."

"So. You gave her the address and told her I had a room before speaking to me?" Melinda tilted her head.

"Something like that. Now, I'm going to go greet her and let her know the bill has been settled."

"Why is she here? You still haven't given me a reason."

Shit. Melinda wouldn't let this rest, and it would eventually come out. At some point, everyone in town would find out that Trinity Hughes was Jeff Allen's daughter.

"She's here to find out some information about her father," Emmett said. He couldn't completely lie to Melinda, but he'd find a way to give her the information piecemeal.

"And she needs your help for that?" Melinda planted her hands on her hips. Her eyes grew wide as that wicked brain of hers turned a million and one possibilities over.

"I'd better go meet her at the front door."

"What the hell have you gotten me into, Emmett Avery Kirby?"

God, he hated when anyone used his full name, but it especially grated on his nerves when his ex did. He closed his eyes and counted to ten before blinking them open once more. "Nothing. It doesn't concern you."

"What has this woman done?"

"Jesus. You think I'd ask you to put up a criminal? I'm a damn cop, for Christ's sake."

"Then why are you being so sketchy? You know I'm not a gossip. I can keep a secret—even for you."

"I need you to let it go, Melinda. Can you do that?"

"For now," she said with a nod. "But if anything weird happens, I'm going to browbeat her until I find out. Got it?"

"Understood." He turned on his heels and double-timed it to the front of the house, pulling open the massive wood doors. "Oh. Hello." He cleared his throat as a woman about five-ten with long, dark hair, blue eyes, and a slender build stood in front of him with a suitcase at her side and a large bag on her shoulder. "Are you Trinity?" It was hard not to stare at such a beautiful woman. Striking, actually. Something about the emotional depth he saw in her eyes made it nearly impossible to unlock his gaze.

"Yes. And you're Emmett. I recognize you from the news." She stretched out her arm.

He took her hand in a firm shake, holding it longer than would likely be considered appropriate. Her skin was silky-soft and warm. He enjoyed the way it slid across his.

"It's nice to meet you," he managed.

"This place is a bed and breakfast? It's a freaking mansion."

"I know. Wait until you see the inside." He lifted her suitcase and carried it to the bottom of the stairs.

"I don't think I can afford this."

"A friend of mine owns it."

"That's what you're calling me these days?" Melinda glided across the living room floor. "Six months ago, he would have introduced me as his biggest mistake."

"I wouldn't go that far," he mumbled.

"Hi. I'm Melinda. Emmett's ex. Welcome to the Landon Lighthouse, and don't worry about the rate. As Emmett said, it's been handled."

"Oh, no. I can't let you—"

"Yes. You can." Emmett placed his hand on the small of her back. "I insist."

"We both do," Melinda said. "Though he hasn't told me why you've come to town." Melinda held up her hand. "And he's asked me to drop it. So, I will."

Occasionally, Melinda did something that surprised him. This was one of those times.

"Why don't I set up some snacks and a bottle of wine outside by the pool?" Melinda said. "You can take her bag to room eight."

"Thanks." He smiled. "Follow me."

Room eight was on the second floor, down the right hallway and all the way at the end. It wasn't the best room, and it was the smallest with only a full-sized bed, but Melinda had said that the bed and breakfast was nearly full. At least the space had a small balcony and a view. Emmett knew that Trinity would be comfortable.

"You and your ex have a decent relationship."

"It's interesting," Emmett admitted.

"How long were you together?"

"Almost six years. Engaged for four."

"Wow. When did it end?" She followed him into the bedroom.

He hoisted her suitcase up onto the luggage rack. "Almost two years ago. She got married last month. Her husband's a good man, and a friend of mine."

"How do you feel about that?"

"Wasn't too thrilled at first, but they're perfect for each other." He ran a hand across the top of his head. "He's a little more inclined to let Melinda do things her way. She's a sweet person, but sometimes it's her way or…hit the highway."

"I have one of those in my life—only I wouldn't say nice things about him," Trinity said. "I could really use that glass of wine if you don't mind."

"Not at all." He waved his hand toward the door and then mentally gave himself a tongue-lashing for watching her ass swing left and right as she sashayed down the staircase. He'd known her for all of ten minutes and already found himself wanting to know everything about her—and not just because he was attracted to her.

Because she carried herself with confidence.

But she *was* hot.

"Melinda puts on a good spread for her guests." He opened the sliders to the outdoor patio. "There's a sheet in your room to fill out and leave for her and the staff, letting them know your daily needs. She'll make sure you get whatever it is, including a nighttime snack like this. Though the wine costs extra." Emmett took the bottle off the table and winked. "Except where you're concerned."

"I want to pay my way."

"Don't worry about it. I want to do this for you." He poured two glasses of wine and handed one to her before settling onto one of the lounge chairs that overlooked the inlet. He missed this part of living with Melinda. But only this bit. He didn't miss living with his ex. He'd gotten over her, though it had taken some time because he had truly loved her—faults and all. "I know you've had a long drive, so if you want to wait to get into everything—"

"No. I want to know what happened." She sat on the edge of her chair and leaned forward. "Please, tell me every detail."

This could end up being a long night.

Trinity tried like hell not to squeeze the wine glass so hard that she broke it. She stared at Emmett, focusing on his kind, blue eyes. They were like big pools of water, welcoming her to go swimming in them. If she could, she'd dive in.

Emmett seemed like the kind of man who cast a safety net wherever he went.

Her phone buzzed in her back pocket. Kathy had been texting and calling all day, driving Trinity crazy. Sometimes, her friend could be overbearing. She'd deal with her later.

"I'm not sure where to begin." Emmett took a sip of his wine.

Neither did Trinity, but words bubbled to her lips. "Did my father seek you out? Was it a chance meeting?" Her mind spun with a million questions, and she couldn't compartmentalize a single thing. It was like she was sixteen all over again and had just found out that her birth father hadn't died but that he was a murderer.

Her life had been turned upside down in a flash.

Two years of therapy and a lot of anger management classes to get her life back on track, but she'd somehow managed to accept that her parents had done what most would have if they'd been in the same boat.

"I believe he saw my police car in the parking lot of the diner and came inside. But I don't know that for sure because he was nervous when he made eye contact with me."

"What did he do next?" Trinity took a long, slow sip of her beverage. A few boats drifted by as they returned from the ocean. The sun settled behind the bridge, and the moon appeared in the evening sky. Her heart pounded in her chest. It had been years since she'd talked with anyone who had come into direct contact with her dad.

Guilt filled her soul.

She shouldn't have given up the search.

"He asked if I would give you a message and the envelope." Emmett sat up, swinging his legs to the side. "Have the FBI or the state police contacted you about what I gave them?"

"No."

"There was a note for you inside. I have a copy of it, but it belongs to you. They should have reached out to you already. If nothing more than to follow up. Hang on a second." He dug into his pocket and pulled out his cell. He tapped on the screen and hit the speaker function.

It rang three times before someone answered.

"This is Agent Robash."

"This is Lieutenant Emmett Kirby with the Lighthouse Cove Police Department. I was wondering if you'd been able to reach Trinity Hughes yet." He lifted his finger to his lips.

"Actually, we have," Robash said. "The family has been notified. I'll be making a statement in the morning."

Trinity opened her mouth, but Emmett reached out and covered it with his hand.

"I'm sorry. You spoke to Trinity?"

"Lieutenant Kirby, we appreciate your due diligence in this, but I have other things that need my attention. Thank you." The phone went dead.

"What the fuck?" Trinity jumped to her feet. Wine sloshed out of the glass and onto her white shirt, but she didn't care. She set it on the small table and patted down her pants pockets, finding her phone. "Nothing. Not a single message." She found the last text string with her parents and quickly typed a note to them, asking if they'd heard anything. "Why would that agent lie?"

"I don't know, but I plan to find out." He took her by the forearms. "Hey. I'm going to get to the bottom of this, don't worry."

"Is that federal agent still in town?"

"She works out of Fort Lauderdale, but that's only an hour south of here. I'll contact her in the morning. If she doesn't respond, I'll go over her head. If that doesn't work, there are other ways to get information from the feds. Trust me."

"Why should I?" Trinity asked.

"Because I'm here and I made a promise to your father before he was killed."

"My father might have killed a man thirty-five years ago, but I know he didn't murder sixteen men over the last two years. It doesn't make any sense."

"I concur," Emmett said. "Please. Will you sit down."

She sucked in a deep breath and let it out slowly. "You said you had a copy of the note. Can I see it?"

"Of course." He took a folded piece of paper out of his pocket. "I printed this off my phone. I shouldn't have done that. I'm usually a by-the-book kind of cop. I mean, my mother is the chief of police and would can my ass if I wasn't because I'd make her look bad. But she knows I did this. So, here you go."

"I don't understand. What did you do that is so bad?"

"I took pictures of the file your dad gave to me to give to you that I had to turn over to the feds."

Trinity laughed. "That was a mouthful."

"I know. I said it."

With a shaky hand, she took the piece of paper

and held it in front of her face, focusing on the first word.

Trinity.

Her heart pounded hard inside her chest. The beats came so fast it was impossible to distinguish where one ended and the next started.

"I spent today doing some research into the murders your father was accused of, and the last six were all in a pattern of him moving north."

A tinge of rage burned her lungs. She did her best to keep that fiery beast inside. "What are you implying?"

"Before I keep talking, I want you to know that I'm going to be very careful in the language I choose. This isn't because I don't believe what your father told me but because I'm a cop, and I deal in facts. Right now, what I see is a trail of dead bodies following your father from town to town."

"Keyword there is *following*."

"Jeff said he didn't know he'd been accused of murdering all those men until he was in a shelter and saw it on television. That was a year ago. That's when he left that town. A month later, there was another murder."

"Don't you find that odd?"

"No. I don't." Emmett scooted to the edge of the

lounge chair. "If I were the detective assigned to this case, I would have come to the same conclusion everyone else has."

"Because of the notes the killer left? Did anyone think to match my father's handwriting?"

"I don't know what the feds or state police are doing because I'm not being kept in the loop. However, I'm having someone look into it." Emmett reached out and rested his hand on her shoulder. "I was raised by a cop. A good one. She taught me to question everything. And while Lighthouse Cove is a quiet, seaside town where not much happens, especially things like murders, she always told me that when crimes like that *do* occur, I should try to prove the opposite of what things appear to be. That way, I can always be sure."

"So, you're saying it's pretty obvious my father killed those men."

"I'm saying it's the obvious conclusion, but that doesn't mean he did it. All it means is that the evidence we have right now points to Jeff Allen. If I were the cop in charge, I'd be looking at trying to prove that he didn't do it, at least to myself. Whenever you go at something from the opposing angle, you often get it right."

"But that implies you're of the mind he's guilty." She turned toward the water and stared at the parade of boat lights coming in from a long day out at sea. The faint sound of music rolled across the air. "My father was forty years old when he was released from prison. Forty-seven when he left Pensacola. That was twenty years ago. These murders have been going on for two years. That doesn't make sense. Serial killers have a need to kill. It's not something they can turn on and off or control. So, if my dad *did* kill all those men, I would think we would have many more bodies over the course of many years."

"I agree. And my mom, brothers, and I are all looking into that."

"Brothers?"

Emmett smiled, and his eyes lit up with pride. He had a way about him that made Trinity feel safe. She wasn't used to that from men.

"I have six. Two of them are cops like me. One is a lawyer, and another is a private investigator. They're all helping out."

"What about the other two?"

"My baby brother, Jamison, is a firefighter. He actually lives a couple of streets down. And my younger brother, Miles, is a mechanic. He owns his own shop. They both have different skill sets but are around if we need them."

"Big family. Are you all close?" She faced him, sucking in a deep breath. The warm, salty air filled her lungs. It had a calming effect.

"We are, but we've had our ups and downs like everyone," he said, pointing to the note in her hands. "Are you avoiding reading that?"

"You're intuitive." Feeling as though some of the anger that had filtered through her system had subsided, she eased back into the chair. "Did my dad tell you I hadn't seen him since I was sixteen?"

"No. He hadn't mentioned that."

"My mom remarried when I was five, and her husband adopted me."

"That means your dad had to give up his parental rights," Emmett said.

She nodded. All the emotions she'd felt as a sixteen-year-old settled in the pit of her stomach, threatening to explode. Heat filled her veins, traveling through her body from her toes to her fingertips. Flashes of her past blackout rage bombarded her mind. For brief moments, she understood how people could be pushed over the edge. Of course, her therapist at the time had told her that she'd been using her anger to try to connect to a man she had no idea existed and to punish her parents.

Now, as an adult, she knew that had been true. Her anger had been a manifestation of pain and betrayal. Now that her father had been shot dead, and the police were closing the case without even considering that the killer could be someone else, it made her blood boil the same way being lied to until she was a teenager had.

"My mom got a really good lawyer and later told me that my father had such guilt that he agreed it was best for me to be raised by Ben."

"How did you find out about your dad?"

"When I was sixteen, he reached out to me after my mother told him not to. He had no idea that my mom had lied to me and told me he was dead."

"That's harsh."

She nodded. "He'd been out of prison for a while, and his probation had ended. He was completely a free man, and he wanted a second chance." Trinity couldn't believe the word vomit coming out of her mouth. She was telling Emmett things she barely told her best friend, and she'd known him for all of maybe an hour.

She leaned over and lifted her wine, giving it a good swirl before taking another gulp. A part of her had no desire to read the note from her dad or to dig into his past.

However, a bigger part of her felt compelled to do so.

"He didn't want to be my father, or so he said, but he wanted to know me. I'd been so angry at everyone that I turned to drugs and became a shitty person. I wanted nothing to do with any of them, and that's when my birth dad disappeared for good."

"You and my brother Jamison should have a chat. What he went through is similar, at least in the sense that he found out our dad isn't his biological father."

"Wow. Really?"

Emmett nodded. "It was quite the scandal in this town, and my brother was pretty angry for a long time. Especially with my mom, who is currently engaged to his biological father." Emmett rubbed his temple. "Every time I explain this, it gives me a headache."

"Do you have a problem with it?"

"No. Not really. I mean, he's my brother. That hasn't changed. And it's not really all that complicated. We all get along now and are one big happy family, but it's weird to say out loud, as I'm sure all of this is for you."

She couldn't argue that point. She raised the

paper for a second time, determined to read it. She'd come all this way to find answers. There was no point in avoiding anything.

Trinity.

I'm sorry. For so many things. I can't change the past, and I want you to know that I take full responsibility for my actions. I live with such regret for what I did. But that is the only bad thing I've done in my life. I didn't do the things I've been accused of. I haven't murdered anyone. And I certainly wouldn't do it in honor of Paul, as those notes the killer left said. Whoever is killing these people is setting me up. He's killing men who are cheating on their wives and making it like I'm still holding a grudge. I'm not. The only thing I hold onto from the past is regret for what I've done and how it affected you. And now it's going to hurt you again. I'm sorry to drag you into this, but I don't know where else to turn. Please don't let these murders tarnish my name even more. I didn't do it.

I've left you a sketch of a man who has been following me for the last six months. He's either the killer, or he's helping him. I need to disappear again because if the police find me, it's going to be shoot to kill.

Trinity gasped. "He didn't stand a chance, did he?"

"Actually, he did. I'm sorry, but he walked out of the diner with a gun in his hands. If he hadn't done that, he might still be alive. I wish I knew why, but he basically ended his life."

She glanced over the note. "That's brutally honest."

"Would you rather I sugarcoat it or lie to you?"

"No. I appreciate you being so upfront." She blew out a short breath and lowered her gaze.

Find someone you can trust. Someone who can help you clear my name.

Jeff. Or Dad. Whichever you prefer.

"That was rough." She swiped at her cheeks. "Sounds like my dad didn't have any fight left in him." Her heart broke into a million pieces. She half-assed trying to find her father for years. Fear had stifled that effort. Now, it was too late.

"He looked as though he'd been living a hard life for a while," Emmett said. "But many homeless people do."

"What else was in that envelope he had for me?"

"I didn't bring the printouts, but here." He held up his cell. "This is the sketch of the man he said was following him. I ran it through our database but got nothing. My brother, Rhett, the private investigator, is trying to find out who the man is. Do you recognize him?"

"No. I can't say that I do." She studied the image but got nothing.

"If you swipe to the next image, it's a ledger of every place Jeff saw that man. Dates. Times. Places. Your dad also started tracking the victims. Unfortunately, that is working against him since he was seen going into libraries and using their computers. He did Google searches on some of the past victims. And that makes him look guilty."

She handed Emmett his phone back. "Where do we start?"

"Well, I'm going to start with the feds. If you're cool with it, I'd like you to meet with my brother Rhett and go over some things with him. Do you think your mom and her husband would be willing to speak with us?"

Trinity nodded. "They want to believe my dad is innocent, but it's a struggle for them sometimes."

"I get it," Emmett said. "One other thing. I don't want you telling anyone about the contents of that envelope. Not even your parents. Can you do that for me?"

"Yes. But why?"

"For starters, if the feds found out, they could make things difficult for me. And my mom. I'm not ready to show my hand yet. If anyone finds out, we've lost our leverage." Emmett glanced at his watch. "I need to get going. Are you going to be all right here?"

"Are you kidding?" She waved her hand toward the inlet. "I'm going to sit here, enjoy the view,"—she raised her wine—"get a little buzzed, and then go to bed."

"Sounds like a plan." He leaned over and tucked a piece of hair behind her ear. It seemed a little too intimate, but she welcomed the human contact. "I'll see you first thing tomorrow. Call me if you need anything." He squeezed her shoulder.

"Thank you doesn't seem good enough."

"I'm just doing my job," Emmett said.

"This goes above and beyond the call of duty."

"Maybe. But every citizen is innocent until proven guilty in a court of law. Not the court of public opinion. Just because your father is dead doesn't mean this case is closed. Not by a long shot."

4

Emmett stood next to his mother outside the town hall and waited for Robash to step behind the podium to give her statement. "Why didn't she invite you? Or me, for that matter? I was there with Jeff Allen when one of her men shot him." Emmett swallowed the bile in his throat. He'd replayed that scene in his head a million times. It kept him up half the night, and he knew for sure that Robash's agent had jumped the gun. "I get this is a national case, but it happened in our town."

"Relax. It's not that big of a deal, and I hate being on television anyway," his mother said. "Besides, what would I say? That I disagree with how she handled the situation? That wouldn't look good, and my boss would have my head."

"I'm glad you agree that Robash mismanaged the scene." Emmett rolled his neck.

"That was obvious. But now she's doing what we would do and covering her office's tracks. For all we know, she's already had words with her agent and is dealing with it. If I were in her shoes, I wouldn't let another department be up there with me. Not when someone fucked up. Too risky. Too much chance of making me look bad."

He had to admit that it made sense. "How long has she been the agent in charge at the Fort Lauderdale office?"

"I think for about four years."

"Have you ever worked with her before?" he asked.

"Nope," his mother said. "We've crossed paths once or twice, but Lighthouse Cove hasn't had a case where we needed the feds or where they wanted in on something. Not since the Rollins killing."

"That was a shitshow," Emmett said. "Here she comes." He folded his arms and widened his stance.

The sound of camera shutters filled his ears. All the reporters present either lifted their microphones and shoved them in Robash's direction or held up recorders if they were magazine or newspaper writers.

"I want to thank everyone for coming," Robash said. "I'd like to start by expressing my gratitude to the Lighthouse Cove Police Department for their help."

"Isn't that sweet?" Emmett muttered. She didn't even mention the chief of police or her son, who spent some time with the accused. But whatever.

"I know the citizens of South Florida have been on edge for the last two years while the *Adultery Killer* was terrorizing our communities. We were on our way here yesterday to arrest Jeff Allen for those murders. The physical evidence is overwhelming in this case. While my office has some paperwork left to finalize, I'm confident that we have caught our man, and so is the district attorney. Thank you, everyone." She turned on her heels and headed straight for her SUV.

Reporters shouted questions after her, but she didn't even glance over her shoulder.

"That's it?" Emmett asked. "That doesn't answer anything, and the reporters are turning and expecting us to answer their questions now."

"Shit," his mother said. "When Robash said she'd handle it, I thought that was exactly what she meant." His mom held up her hands. "Sorry, folks. My office has no comment."

"Come on, Chief," Jon Kaplan said. "You've got to give us something. A man was gunned downed in a local diner, and you've got nothing to say about it?"

"This is the FBI's case. They are handling everything," his mother said.

"What about you, Emmett? You were there," Kaplan said. "Can you shed some light on what happened and why the FBI was so quick to—?"

"All questions need to be directed to Agent Robash and her team," Emmett said. "Now, if you will excuse us." Emmett took his mother by the arm and guided her through the crowd and into the building where the police department was located.

A few reporters hollered after them, but no one followed.

No one dared.

Besides, they knew better. They wouldn't get anything out of either of them at this point. But that didn't mean they wouldn't come knocking.

"What the hell was that woman thinking?" His mother pulled out her cell and tapped the screen. "If she thinks she's going to drive away and leave things like that, she's got another thing coming."

"Put it on speaker."

His mother tapped the appropriate space on the screen.

"This is Agent Robash."

As if she couldn't tell who was calling.

"This is Police Chief Rebecca Kirby. Care to tell me why you gave a non-statement?"

"I'm sorry," Robash said. "I've got an urgent situation with another case. I had to go. But there is nothing else to say until I get the permission to close the case, anyway, which I'm expecting to happen tomorrow afternoon."

"How can you—?"

"Sorry, I've got to go." Robash ended the call.

"This doesn't make sense," his mother said. "Didn't you tell me that she lied about speaking with the daughter of the accused?"

"Flat-out lied, and Trinity was sitting next to me. She heard the entire thing."

"I don't like that, Emmett." His mother shook her head. "She shouldn't be that close to this case. Especially when we're questioning how well a federal agent handled an investigation."

"Mom, she has a right to know."

"I'm not disagreeing. And you know I'd tell her. Just not right away." His mom reached out and tapped her palm against his cheek.

He jerked his head away. He hated it when she did that in the office. It was bad enough that she did it at all. Especially considering that he was a grown man and not a child.

She smiled and let out a slight laugh. "Are you going to see this Trinity now? Are you being a gentleman?"

"Of course, I am."

"I saw a picture of her. She's beautiful and very much your type, at least in that department."

"I have a type?"

"Yeah. The damsels in distress."

"That's really not funny," he said. "But, speaking of that, I put Trinity up at Melinda's."

His mother lowered her chin and arched a brow. "How does Melinda feel about that?"

"She doesn't know who she is, not really, but she'll figure it out. And she'll be kind."

"Of course, she will. Of all the people in this town, she'll understand. But that's not the point. She has a business to run. She has a right to know who's staying at her place. If she has a problem with it, Trinity can stay with Steve and me. Trust me, our place is so huge, she'll get lost. I know I do. Unless you end up becoming her hero."

"Seriously, Mom. Stop." Flashes of Trinity popped into his mind. Of course, they'd been doing that ever since he'd left her last night. He couldn't deny that his body had reacted the second he laid eyes on her. But so what? There were a lot of attractive women out there, and he didn't pursue them. "Why are you all of a sudden teasing me about a woman I just met? You haven't tried to set me up with anyone in months. Why her?"

His mom shrugged. "I don't know. She's got kind eyes."

"You haven't even met her."

"You don't date enough. I think it's time you get back out there. If she's single and interested, why not start there?"

"I'll keep that in mind."

"Good," his mom said. "Now, before I forget, are you going to bring Rhett into this?"

"You know I am."

His mom nodded. "Keep me in the loop."

"I will."

"And don't you dare go and do something I'll have to take your badge for. I expect Nathan to pull that shit. Not you."

"Yes, ma'am"

She waggled her finger. "I mean it. I know you, and you have that look in your eye like when you were fifteen and one of the deputies ran over Miles' bike and lied about it. You've always been a rule-follower. Until those who make the rules and are supposed to protect them break them. Remember whose son you are."

"As if I could forget." He chuckled as he headed out of the town hall. Time to head over to the bed and breakfast. He wished he had more to share with Trinity, but maybe Rhett's excellent private investigative skills would uncover something useful.

Until then, he'd spend some time interviewing Trinity and doing his best to keep his mind out of the gutter.

"Did you sleep well?"

Trinity took the mug of coffee that Melinda offered, wishing she could have answered that honestly. "Yes. This place is amazing."

"I'm so glad," Melinda said. "There's a continental breakfast set up in the kitchen, but if you want eggs, pancakes, or anything else, just let my staff know. They can whip you up just about anything. Breakfast is served until ten."

"Thanks. I think I'll just go grab a bagel and sit outside. I've got some phone calls to make."

"No problem. Let me know if you need anything."

Trinity stepped into the kitchen, and a dozen scents assaulted her all at once. Cinnamon. Sugar. Chocolate. Coffee. Maple Syrup. And more. Her stomach flipped over, demanding food.

A mother holding an infant while gently bouncing waited for a man to butter her toast at one of the stations.

Memories flooded Trinity's mind. She flattened a hand over her belly. There had been no cries—only Trinity's tears.

"We'll be out of your way in a jiffy," the man said.

"No worries. I'm going to snag a couple of these chocolate croissants." She lifted two off the tray and put them on a paper plate. Taking her mug and food, she headed outside.

Seeing babies didn't usually trigger that kind of reaction anymore. At least not that strongly. But every once in a while, it brought her right back to that moment. Perhaps it was because of what'd just happened to her biological father. Who knew? Whatever it was, she needed to push those painful memories from her mind. She didn't talk to many people about that part of her past. It was too painful, and most people either didn't understand or said stupid shit.

She picked a lounge chair off to the far side of the pool. After getting herself situated, she called her friend Kathy, who picked up on the first ring."

"Hey, hon. How are you doing?" Kathy asked in a sweet, high-pitched voice. Sometimes, her positive vibe could be annoying, especially when Trinity wanted to wallow in self-pity. Of course, Kathy would never let her do that, which was probably why she'd called her in the first place.

"I'm currently sitting poolside staring at a lighthouse and a bunch of boats going out and coming into the inlet."

"Oh. That sounds so Zen. Did you do some morning yoga?"

Trinity groaned. She should lie, but she couldn't do that to Kathy. "No," she admitted. "I'll get to it."

"You'd better. It will help you through all of this. Of course, I think you should come home. I really don't know why you're there. I take it you saw the morning news?"

"I did," Trinity said. "I can't believe they're wrapping this up so quickly. It doesn't make sense." It also hadn't sat well with her that the chief of police hadn't made a statement, nor did Emmett. But she'd give them a chance to explain themselves.

"Have you met with that police officer? What's his name? Emery?"

"Emmett," Trinity corrected. Sometimes, Kathy could be so ditsy. "I've barely had a chance to talk with him. I'm going to meet him in a couple of hours."

"If he had anything helpful, I bet he would have spilled it right away," Kathy said. "I'm not saying this to be mean, and I don't want to hurt your feelings, but you're wasting your time."

Kathy could very well be right, but Trinity wouldn't be able to live with herself if she didn't at least try to get some answers. She owed it to her dad.

And she needed her friends to support her whether they agreed with her or not. "I don't care if you understand or agree. I need to do this."

"Okay," Kathy said with an exasperated sigh. "But based on the statements the federal agents made on the news, it looked like they were packing up and closing the case."

Emmett had only told her not to talk about the contents of the envelope. He hadn't said that she couldn't discuss anything else.

"Emmett went to the press briefing. He was

going to try to speak with the agent in charge to find out all the particulars."

"That happened like an hour ago. I know you want someone to tell you there was a mistake, but, sweetie, there wasn't. They had the FBI, the state police, and the locals all working together. The evidence is there. Come home. I know this is hard, but you're strong. You'll get through it," Kathy said with her over the top positive attitude she'd had for as long as Trinity had known her—which had been for about a year. It was one of the reasons that Trinity had been drawn to Kathy. Who didn't want a friend that constantly lifted you up and gave you affirmations? Especially when it was a woman.

Only, right now, Trinity needed someone to support her decision, not tell her to give up.

"I can't yet. Not until I feel as if I've done everything I can," Trinity said. "I'm sorry, Kathy. I've got to go. Emmett is here."

"Call me later. Promise?"

"I will." She set the phone on the small table next to her and gave a little wave toward Emmett.

He flashed a wicked smile as he strolled across the patio with his hands stuffed into his pockets.

Her stomach roiled.

Damn, the man reminded her of a movie star

with his dark hair and perfectly straight teeth—and she imagined six-pack abs under that form-fitting T-shirt.

"Sorry it took me so long to get here." He pulled up a chair. "I take it you saw Robash's pathetic excuse for a press conference?"

"I did. Why didn't you or your mom say anything?"

"We were told that more would be said. Robash played my mom. The real question is why."

"Did you ask why she lied to you last night?" Trinity swung her feet to the side and sat up taller.

"No. She didn't give me a chance."

That old sensation of heat rising from the pit of her gut to her eyes began. It wasn't a good feeling. It was more like someone poked her with a cattle prod in her heart, and the searing pain seeped into her veins, poisoning the rest of her body.

"Maybe I should give her a call. Or, better yet, show up at her office."

Emmett rested his hand over her wrist. "I plan on going there tomorrow. I've already learned that she has meetings in the morning, so a surprise visit is in order."

"I want to go." She braced herself, waiting for him to tell her no. The last thing she needed was some man telling her what she could and couldn't do. When she found out the truth at sixteen and went to see her biological father on her own, Ben had hit the roof. Her mother had been even worse, but it had been her adoptive father who'd forbidden her from ever seeing Jeff again. It wasn't so much that her parents had said the word *no*—she'd heard that a million times growing up. Her parents' job was to protect her, and even then, she could understand that they were only trying to do what they thought was best.

The problem was the way Ben had denied her. The animosity that'd spewed from his mouth had been laced with the venom of a hundred rattlesnakes. What Trinity hadn't known at the time was that Ben, the man whom she'd called *Dad* for most of her life, a dedicated medical technician, had been one of the first responders on the scene. He'd seen first-hand the devastation her biological father had caused.

He'd also been the one to scoop her up from her crib and console her because her mother had gone into shock.

"I was going to ask you to come," he said. "I only ask that you follow a few ground rules."

"I might be able to do that."

"Fair enough," he said. "So, how is Melinda treating you?"

"She and her staff are amazing. I can't complain. Thank you so much for setting me up with this."

"It's my pleasure," he said. "So, I'm having my brother Rhett check into some things for us, but it's going to take some time. I thought maybe we could go to the seafood festival tonight if you're up for it. There are some great food trucks along with some good cover bands."

"I could be down for some entertainment."

"Perfect. I'll pick you up around seven." He leaned over and kissed her cheek. His lips lingered a little longer than what would be considered appropriate for two people who'd just met, especially since she was there asking for his police expertise, but who was she to complain?

He had really nice lips.

He jerked back and stared at her with wide eyes. "Sorry. That was inappropriate. Not sure why I did that, other than to say I feel as if I've known you for a while."

"It's okay." She swallowed, her heart beating fast.

He raised his hands. "I promise to be a gentleman tonight."

"I'll see you later." She fanned herself as he turned

and strolled across the patio, passing Melinda along the way.

Two minutes later, Melinda scurried in Trinity's direction and plopped her adorable butt in the chair. "Was my ex flirting with you?"

"Nope," she said.

"O-M-G. He was. That devil." Melinda leaned back and adjusted her sunglasses. "It's been so long since he's dated. He needs to get out more."

This was not a conversation Trinity was having with Melinda. Or anyone. She did not plan on dating Emmett—or anyone for that matter. Not anytime soon anyway.

"I think it's sweet that you and Emmett have a decent friendship after being in a relationship, but that's not why I'm here."

"Ugh." Melinda glanced at her phone. "We'll have that conversation later. For now, I have to deal with some bed and breakfast business. If you need anything at all, snag someone from my staff."

"Thanks." Now, all Trinity had to do was kill time and not think about spending the evening with Emmett.

5

Emmett stuffed his hands into his pockets to keep from lacing his fingers with Trinity's. He found her to be not only insanely attractive but incredibly intelligent, as well.

"You have to try the lobster roll from this one truck. They have the lobster flown in fresh from Maine every day. It's amazing."

"Sounds fantastic. I'd love one," Trinity said.

"Why don't you go grab us a couple of beers and a table under the tent? I'll get them and some fries." He pointed toward the picnic area. "The line is pretty long. You'll probably get the beers much faster, so get four." He handed her forty bucks."

"Sounds like a plan."

He stood in line while he glanced over his shoulder at least a dozen times, checking Trinity out.

There were so many things to like about her and a million reasons he shouldn't get involved. He nearly laughed out loud. What made him think she'd be interested in him? Just because she was out at the seafood festival? She had nothing else to do while they waited to head to Fort Lauderdale tomorrow.

And the only reason she was in Lighthouse Cove to begin with was because an FBI agent had gunned down her father in front of a diner.

"Hey, big brother." The sound of Jamison's voice cut through the night air.

Emmett turned. "Yo. What's up?"

Jamison had Zadie in one of those baby contraptions that kept her tight to his chest. "Same thing you are." He slapped Emmett on the back.

Bryn, Jamison's wife, stood close by, rubbing her growing belly.

"Look at you," Emmett said. "You're getting bigger every time I see you."

"Thanks for the reminder." Bryn patted her belly. "Not only am I getting fat, but this little fella, and we did find out it's a boy, likes playing soccer on my bladder."

"Congratulations." Emmett leaned in and kissed

Bryn on the cheek. He was truly happy for his brother and his wife. Though he'd be lying if he said his heart didn't hurt a tad. For the most part, he'd been able to move past his pain, but every once in a while, he had moments where his soul grabbed hold of those memories and tormented his mind. "A bouncing baby boy. That's awesome."

"Who are you here with?" Jamison asked. "Mom mentioned that you were helping the daughter of the man who the feds shot. Did you bring her?"

"Yes," Emmett admitted. "What the hell has Mom been saying?" The line went from ten to eight. It shouldn't be too long now.

"Only that Melinda said she's really pretty."

"Fucking wonderful," Emmett muttered.

Jamison covered Zadie's ears. "Hey. Small child present."

"She's only a few months old. She's not picking up her uncle's bad mouth," Emmett said. "But I'll work on it."

"You better." Bryn playfully smacked his shoulder. "Now, point out your friend. I need to take a load off."

"She's the one with the long, brown hair over there." Emmett pointed.

"Perfect. I'll go introduce myself." Bryn kissed her

little girl's forehead before rising on tiptoe and smacking her lips against her husband's. "I'll try not to embarrass you too much."

"Gee. Thanks for that." Emmett knew that Bryn was mostly teasing; however, she'd jumped on the let's-fix-up-Emmett bandwagon lately. He waited until she was out of earshot before saying more. "Seriously, what the hell is Mom saying? Because I don't need this shit right now. Between trying to understand what happened with Jeff Allen and—"

"Relax, big brother," Jamison said. "Mom is honestly more concerned that you're going to fall head over heels in love with a woman who isn't available. And, honestly, Trinity seems like just the type."

"Why the hell would you say that? And if you mention the damsel in distress crap, I'll pop you."

Jamison laughed as he patted his little girl's bottom. "It's not that. And Melinda wasn't even close to being a damsel in distress. That chick's a fighter, and I bet Trinity is, too."

"Then what?" Emmett moved closer to the order station. "Because I don't get how anyone can say that when I'm the only one who's met her."

"Melinda's met her. And let's remember that

Mom has a weird obsession with being close to our exes, even when *we* don't want to be."

"That's true," Emmett said. "So, what you're saying is that I need to have words with Melinda."

"Melinda is no Cheryl. She honestly just wants you to be happy and has no idea who Trinity is. Yet. But give that girl another day or two, and she'll put it all together."

"I know. I am worried about that."

"Maybe you should tell her before she finds out on her own," Jamison said.

"I need a couple of days. Rhett is doing his thing, and I'm heading to Fort Lauderdale tomorrow. I need to know why Robash is lying."

"Do you think Trinity's dad murdered those men?" Jamison asked in a hushed tone.

"Actually, no. I don't. But I also don't have access to all the hard evidence. So, I could be talking out of my ass."

"I trust your instincts," Jamison said. "What does Mom think?"

"That this case stinks, and that Jeff Allen got a raw deal."

Trinity glanced up at the sky and stared at the stars and the moon. She'd always loved living in Florida, but something about South Florida was extra-special. It was different than Pensacola. It was almost magical. The moon was brighter, and the stars dotted the endless sky, lighting it up like a Christmas tree.

She could get used to living in a place like Lighthouse Cove.

She brought the light beer to her lips and eyed a pregnant woman as she approached with a smile.

"Trinity?" the woman asked.

"Yes. And you are?"

"Bryn. I'm Jamison's wife. Jamison is one of Emmett's brothers." Bryn took a seat at the table. "Sorry to intrude, but my feet are killing me, and this baby is kicking the hell out of my insides."

"No worries," Trinity said. "How far along are you?"

"Six months. It's my second one, and at this rate, my last one," she said. "We want more, but we'll adopt the next."

"Are you serious?" Trinity's voice screeched, and her pulse increased. "I'm sorry. That sounded rude." There was no way a stranger could know that conversation was a hot button for her or that it would trigger a shit-ton of emotions.

"Not at all. And, yes. I'm serious. Both Jamison and I love the idea of adopting. To make a very long story short, we believe that, sometimes, the best families aren't created the old-fashioned way."

"I think that's beautiful."

"So do we." Bryn stretched out her legs, crossing her ankles. "Looks like the boys are next in line. I'm so freaking hungry, I think I could eat two lobster rolls."

"Emmett looks so different from Jamison," Trinity commented.

"They have different fathers," Bryn said. "Jamison looks like his biological father, while Emmett favors his biological father. It's all a bit confusing at first, but we're one big happy family now."

"This might be a strange question, but is that why you're interested in adopting?" For Trinity to ever have a family, she'd have to adopt. But she was thirty-six years old. She wasn't a spring chicken. And who didn't want to have a child of their own? Even Jamison and this woman were having one together. And she had two naturally, so it wasn't like adoption was their only chance at a family. They had choices—unlike Trinity.

"There are a million reasons we want to adopt. One is that we want to have a large family, and neither of us is getting any younger. And another is that Jamison does a lot of volunteer work with an orphanage. He sees kids that need a good home every day. He'd like to adopt an older child, and I'm totally on board with that. We're even talking about fostering. We're not exactly sure what we're going to do yet, but as soon as this little guy is born, and we've adjusted to having two kids, we're going to start the paperwork."

"That's cool. A lot of people would shy away from that."

"My Jamison isn't a lot of people." Bryn smiled, her eyes twinkling. "He brings out the best in everyone, and I'm lucky to love him."

"I'd say he's the lucky one."

Bryn leaned closer. "I wouldn't disagree."

"Here they come," Trinity said. She needed to be done with the conversation. While she was truly happy and excited for Bryn and Jamison, Trinity felt her chest tighten after a while whenever there was a ton of baby talk. And with everything else going on, her emotions were all over the place. "Holy crap. Those lobster rolls are huge."

"They sure are. And they're amazing. We know

the guy who owns the truck. He only ships in the best. You're going to love it," Bryn said.

"Hey, babe." Jamison set a tray of food on the table before sitting in a chair, all while dealing with a fussy baby like a pro. "Eat up before this one decides she's hungrier than her mama."

"I can feed her and eat at the same time," Bryn said.

"But you don't have to." Jamison tugged at the side of the contraption that held his daughter against his chest. "However, she's about to go full-on cry on us."

"Just give her to me. But you might have to feed me while I feed our daughter."

"I have no problem doing that," Jamison said.

Trinity turned her head as she shoved her face full of lobster roll. "Wow. This is amazing." Thank goodness she had something else to focus on; otherwise, she might break down and cry.

"I know, right?" Emmett said. "So, you've met Bryn, and this is my brother, Jamison."

"His much younger brother, for the record." Jamison winked as he passed his daughter to Bryn, who covered herself with a small blanket before breastfeeding her child.

It amazed Trinity how at ease both Jamison and

Bryn were at being parents. Of course, they'd had months of practice, but still, Trinity had seen other people fumbling their way through things.

"Jamison here is the baby of the family. And he doesn't let a moment go by without reminding any of us of that fact."

"I'm an only child," Trinity said. "I've always wondered what it would be like to have siblings."

"I have a sister. She's my best friend," Bryn said. "These two are from a family of seven boys. And they are all close. I want that for my kids. It's pretty amazing."

"I imagine it is." Trinity sucked in a breath, hoping she held back all her emotion. She lifted the lobster roll and took a big bite. "I don't think I've ever had anything that tasted this great."

"It's the best." Emmett placed his hand on her thigh and squeezed. "Why don't we finish up here and head back to the bed and breakfast?"

"Sounds good to me."

It was as if he'd read her mind, and that was something she appreciated. It also scared her because the last thing she needed was to be connected to a man in less than a day.

6

Emmett leaned against the hood of his personal SUV and waited for his brother, Rhett, who was late—which was normal. Emmett tried to keep his frustration in check as he sipped his coffee, but no matter how often he practiced a little Zen breathing and thinking, Rhett had a way of making Emmett lose his cool.

He glanced at his watch.

Only five minutes late.

Okay, maybe it wasn't Rhett who'd gotten Emmett all riled up. Perhaps it could be a long, sleepless night and the fact that he'd had to take a cold shower because a certain female had occupied his mind all night.

It had been a long time since a woman had gotten under his skin this way.

Emmett blew out a puff of air before downing the last of his bitter brew and starting in on the special blend he'd brought for his brother. Fuck it. He'd understand, and if he didn't…oh, well.

Unfortunately, the coffee wasn't all that hot anymore. Emmett tapped his foot against the pavement, doing his best to rid himself of his irritation.

The sound of a motorcycle caught Emmett's attention. He glanced over his shoulder and sighed.

He wasn't going to share. Not today.

Emmett did his best to chug the coffee.

Rhett screeched to a stop. He kicked the stand, rested the bike on it, then lifted his big, black helmet off his head. "Hey, bro. How ya doing?"

"I'm fucking annoyed. Why can't you be on time at least once in your life?"

"Mom says I'll be late for my funeral." Rhett narrowed his eyes. "But I'm not really late."

"If I had to wait, I consider that late." Emmett really shouldn't take this out on his Irish twin, but they'd been doing this kind of shit since they were toddlers.

Rhett pointed to the empty cup on the hood of the vehicle. "Is one of those for me?"

"It was, but since you were late, I drank it."

"Of course, you did." Rhett let out an exasperated sigh. "But it wasn't because I pulled up about eight minutes past our designated time of arrival." He set his protective headgear on the back of his bike and took off his leather jacket, which he never rode without, no matter the weather. He'd fallen once and had ripped the hell out of his back, so now he wanted that added layer of protection.

Emmett had told him to get rid of the bike, but the moment Krista walked out of Rhett's life ten years ago, Rhett had developed a bit of a daredevil personality and enjoyed pushing the limits; doing things like jumping from perfectly good airplanes.

Why anyone would want to go hurtling toward Earth while holding onto a string and pulling at the last second, hoping that a flimsy piece of fabric would open and save them from landing face-down in the dirt like a raindrop going splat was beyond Emmett.

Of course, of all the kids, Emmett was considered the least likely to break the rules and do anything dangerous, which was an oxymoron since he was a cop and did something that could potentially take his life every time he strapped on his weapon and got in his police car. But whatever. He let his family tease him because they all had their quirks.

"I bet it had something to do with Trinity. Jamison said the two of you made for a cute couple. He agrees with Mom."

"I'm not having this conversation with you." Emmett shook his head. "I know you haven't had much time, but did you find anything out?"

Their mother had been disappointed that Rhett opted to stay in the private sector. She'd always believed he would make a wicked detective, and Emmett had to agree. His brother's deductive skills were better than anyone else's in their family. He had an uncanny ability to see things in ways no one else could. It was amazing to watch how he solved puzzles.

"That federal agent, Jenna Robash, is an interesting character, but I suppose you know that," Rhett started. "She's got a reputation for being a real hard-ass. She's notorious for getting stuff done and runs a tight ship. Everybody in the department respects her, but she butts heads with many people. My buddy up in the DC office used to work with her and said she doesn't take critiques well from those below her or not in her world. If you're not her boss or someone who can help her career, your opinion doesn't matter. And she begged to have the Adultery Killer case for two months before her boss agreed to give it to her."

"Who had it before her?"

"An agent out of the Miami field office by the name of Frank Cotania."

"That's where the killings started." Emmett pinched the bridge of his nose. "Was Cotania screwing up or something? Were their complaints about his performance or how he was handling the case?"

"That's just it," Rhett said. "From what I've been told, Cotania was doing a fine job and has an exemplary record. When the Miami Police Department found a fifth body that fit the killer's profile, they decided to ask the FBI for help. They worked closely with Cotania, who doesn't take over like Robash does. He prefers to play nice with the locals, though he still likes being the boss. I haven't spoken to him yet, but I was thinking I might take a ride to Miami today. It's always better to talk to these people face-to-face."

"Agreed." While Emmett had never worked in a big office, he understood that every law enforcement officer wanted that one case that could make their career. Generally speaking, it wasn't about making a name for oneself, at least not in the public eye, but about proving to yourself and your superiors that not only did you have what it took, but also that you would always bring it.

That way, you'd get the next assignment over someone else.

But taking a case mid-stream from someone else took balls.

Arrogance.

Ambition.

It also alienated a person from their colleagues.

"Robash told me point-blank last night that she'd spoken to Trinity, only she hadn't. So, I made an appointment to meet with the agent. Only she doesn't know I'm bringing Trinity with me."

"Sneaky bastard," Rhett teased as he pulled a folder out of the satchel on the back of his bike. "I did some studying of the crime scenes, and something doesn't add up with this being a homeless guy killing because he doesn't like cheaters."

"What's that?"

"First, it seems the killer spends a little time torturing the victims. I can't be sure until I have this analyzed, and then I'm hopeful Cotania can confirm my suspicions, but I believe whoever murdered these men was military. And Jeff never served."

"Can you be a little more specific on why you think that?"

"The autopsy pictures I was able to get show torture tactics that only the military use, and we're not talking your average military man. I'm talking special forces or black ops." Rhett opened the folder and handed Emmett a piece of paper. "It appears the police and feds kept the torture from the media, along with a few other details. It only got buried deeper when Robash took over."

"How long after she became lead on the Adultery Killer case did she hone in on Jeff Allen as the suspect?"

"That's how she got the case," Rhett said. "She figured out the Paul connection when an anonymous tip came in about a person looking like Jeff where one of the bodies was found. The weird thing, though, was that her office took the call, not Cotania's. The only answer I have for that is that the caller phoned in on the national hotline and got sent to the wrong field office."

"Sounds a little too contrived." Emmett didn't believe in coincidences. "But why would Robash go that far out of her way to get a case?"

"I don't know. But there's more. Look at the kills." Rhett pointed to one of the autopsy images. "Whoever murdered these people used a military-grade knife. Another thing that was kept from the media. In Cotania's original notes, he stated he was looking into displaced local veterans."

"Once again, Jeff doesn't fit that description."

"Maybe that sketch he made does," Rhett said.

"Trinity sent it to her family and some people from her father's past, but nothing turned up."

"I have to ask, how is Melinda taking having Trinity stay at her place?"

"Melinda hasn't made the connection yet. Or if she has, she's not freaking out." Emmett glanced over his shoulder. The sun beamed down on the big, white house with its green shutters. A few of the guests stepped from the front door and scurried down the walkway toward the street, heading into town. The nice thing about the location of the Landon Lighthouse Bed and Breakfast was the ability to walk to restaurants, stores, and some of the other great attractions Lighthouse Cove had to offer. "I hope she doesn't, but you know Melinda. She's one smart cookie. Mom thinks I should tell her, and soon."

"Even if she does know, unless her husband is

uncomfortable with the situation, she's not going to make a big deal of Trinity staying there, or tell the town she's the daughter of an accused serial killer."

Emmett could only hope.

"So, is Trinity as hot in person as she is in the pictures I've seen?"

"Not your type," Emmett said with a little more bite to his words than necessary. His brother didn't treat women badly—far from it, actually. But he couldn't commit to anyone for more than a few months. If that. He was always upfront and honest with the girls he dated. However, he was still madly in love with Krista. That meant there was always a third person in any relationship Rhett had, and that never ended well.

He'd completely given Krista his heart, and she'd broken it. He'd never allow that to happen again.

Emmett could understand that emotion because there had been times right after his breakup with Melinda that he wasn't sure if he could ever let himself fall in love again. But the more that wound healed, the more he realized he didn't want to be alone for the rest of his life. Only, it was hard to trust again.

"Everyone's my type. You're the picky one," Rhett said. "Mom and Dad think I'm pining for a woman who's never going to show her face in this town again, but they're wrong. Still, maybe it's you who's still got a flame cooking for an ex." He pointed to the bed and breakfast. "Of all the places you could have put a guest from out of town."

"Not that I have to explain myself to you, but she had a room, and she gave it to us dirt-cheap," Emmett said through a clenched jaw. "I'm over Melinda. And stay away from Trinity. She just lost a father she never got the chance to know and she's hurting. She doesn't need you hitting on her."

"But it's okay if you do." Rhett held his hands up. "Don't try to say you weren't. Even Bryn thinks it's only a matter of time."

Fucking wonderful. Emmett's entire family was talking about him and Trinity. This was the last thing he needed. "I'm not doing anything of the sort."

"You're telling me to back off. I can count on one hand the times you've told me to do that, and it's always when you're interested in asking a girl out." Rhett arched a brow. "She's gotten under your skin. I know you, bro, so don't try to tell me she hasn't."

"Not the point."

"It's exactly the point. And there's nothing wrong with getting to know her."

"The timing is all wrong."

"That's not what you said when you and Melinda hooked up." Rhett grabbed his helmet and smiled. "I'll call you when I get back from Miami."

"Be safe."

"I always am." He flipped up the kickstand and revved the engine before easing out onto the street and taking off.

Emmett rubbed the back of his neck and stared into the big picture window where he saw Trinity sitting at the breakfast nook, having a cup of coffee. She'd pulled her long hair into a braid that cascaded down her back. She palmed the mug and brought it to her plump lips.

Shit.

Emmett needed to get his head on straight. Trinity needed his help clearing her father's name. She didn't need him trying to get her into his bed.

Emmett jogged around the hood of his SUV. He didn't quite make it to the passenger side to open the door for Trinity, but he was able to offer his hand.

"Thank you," she said.

"My pleasure." He closed the door and pressed

the handle, looking at the vehicle. "Remember what I said on the drive down."

"To let you do most of the talking and follow your lead, and that whatever I do, don't become antagonistic."

He rested his hand on the small of her back. "Or sarcastic or have a tone like you do right now."

"I'm normally not this hotheaded. Really. I'm not. It's just that I can't believe a federal agent would lie to a fellow officer. I don't understand what's going on, and it's making me ornery."

"I get it." If he were in her shoes, he'd be pissed as hell. "But we need Robash to believe we're not pushing her buttons, yet we're not willing to be pushovers."

"She lied, Emmett. And she's acting like this is a slam dunk. How can we trust anything she says?" Trinity mumbled. "No offense, but it makes me not trust any of you."

"I know." Emmett let out a long breath. There was an occasional justification for lying to family members and victims of crimes.

But he couldn't, for the life of him, come up with a valid reason for why Robash had lied to a fellow law enforcement officer about speaking to Trinity. That didn't make sense.

Emmett signed them in at the front desk, and they made their way to security where he registered his gun and set it on the conveyor belt along with his badge and wallet, while Trinity emptied her purse into a bin. She walked through the metal detector first.

Then Emmett.

Neither one beeped.

He holstered his weapon and headed toward the elevator with his hand placed firmly on Trinity's back. "The guard already called up to Robash. I'll bet you five bucks she's waiting for us when we get off the elevator."

"You think she's that anxious to see us?"

"Not to see us but to get rid of us, especially since we're here without an appointment." Emmett pressed the button five times as if that would make the damn thing come any sooner.

Federal buildings always made him nervous, which was stupid. He was a cop. But still. It didn't matter that his mother generally worked well with all law enforcement agencies. His mom, as the chief of police, had to be more of a diplomat.

Emmett didn't.

And he didn't like playing nice in the sandbox with people like Robash.

The FBI's office was on the third floor of the federal building. This field office had ten agents, and Robash was the agent in charge of violent crimes. She had a team of three, but rumor had it that she wasn't easy to work with or for.

Emmett stared at the numbers inside the elevator as it lurched upward in a jerky motion.

"I hate these things," Trinity whispered. "I'm always afraid I'm going to get stuck in one."

"You met Jamison. He's broken a few people out of these things. It's not that horrible."

"That doesn't make me feel better."

The doors slid open, and there stood Robash, wearing a pair of dark slacks and a dark shirt. One of her men stood next to her, and he didn't look all that thrilled to be there.

"I'm surprised you drove all this way to see me when you could have called," Robash said as she eyed Trinity. "And you brought someone else from your department. I'm beginning to feel like this is an ambush."

"I wouldn't say that," Emmett said. Let the games begin. "This is Trinity Hughes."

Robash's eyes grew wide.

"She's Jeff Allen's biological daughter, and she'd like copies of everything in the envelope her father left for her—which he instructed me to give to her, and you mentioned you spoke to her about."

"No." Robash narrowed her eyes. "All I said was that the family had been notified, which is true." She wiggled her finger in Emmett's direction. "Don't try to misconstrue my words."

"I wouldn't dare do that." Emmett took Trinity's hand and squeezed. They had spoken to her mom on the drive down. Yes, Jenna Robash had called to inform the family that Jeff Allen was dead and gave them a big fat sorry about him being a serial killer. But that was it. Nothing about the envelope. "I must have heard wrong. However, there is still the issue of the envelope that Jeff wanted his daughter to have, and we're here to collect it."

"I'm sorry. That's part of our investigation. I can't release it," Robash said. "This case might be nearly closed, but I need to preserve evidence for years. You know that."

"Doesn't mean you can't get a family member copies of personal things. Jeff told me there was a note for Trinity in there. She has a right to read it."

"I'm sorry. There was no note to Trinity." Robash leaned closer. "May we talk in private?"

"Whatever you have to say, you can say in front of Trinity." Emmett continued holding Trinity's hand, rubbing his thumb over her soft skin. He told himself he was lending her support as a friend. That this was him being a kind, decent person.

Not a man who found himself having feelings he shouldn't.

"The only items in that envelope were things helping us to close this case neatly." Robash widened her stance and folded her arms. "I don't know why he wanted his child to have it unless he was trying to hide the evidence. Would she have protected him? Would she have helped him hide from the police? Would you have helped her?" Robash glanced down at their entangled hands.

"Excuse me?" Trinity took a step forward.

Emmett tugged at her arm. "No. All she wants is to see what was in the envelope. It's not that big of an ask."

"I can tell you it was a list of his kills. Names. Dates. Times and places. Specific things about each victim like what they were wearing and things they said right before they died. It was quite detailed."

That was not what Emmett had seen in that package. Not even close. And he had pictures to prove it.

"I'd like to see that," he said.

"I can have my office send copies to yours as a

courtesy, but again, there was no note for his daughter. He must have been playing games with you. Trying to buy time or something," Robash said. "Was there anything else you needed to see us about? Because I've got a lot to do today."

"I'd like to go through all the evidence you have," Emmett said.

"Why?" Robash shifted her weight. "We've done a thorough investigation. We had more than enough to go to trial, and we would have gotten a conviction." It appeared as though Robash tried to soften her look as she glanced in Trinity's direction. "I know this must be hard for you to hear, and I'm truly sorry. However, there is no reasonable doubt in this case. Jeff Allen murdered all those victims, and we proved it. Case closed."

Time to take a sidebar. Emmett let go of Trinity's hand and took five steps to his right.

Robash followed.

He glanced over his shoulder before leaning closer to Robash.

"My office could learn from this case, and since I was there when he was taken down, I want to know all the details," he said softly. "And, to be honest, if someone Trinity knows and trusts looks everything over and tells her the same thing you just did..." He did his best to act as if he were tired of the whole thing. "We both know what really happened. I need to help her accept it and move on."

"I'll make sure you get a summary of my notes, and you can access the database. If you need anything else, give me a call."

"Thanks. I appreciate your time," he said louder. He wrapped his arm around Trinity's waist and guided her back into the elevator. "I have to admit, I was impressed by your ability to stay quiet," he said once the doors were closed.

"You and me both." She leaned against the steel wall and blew out a puff of air. "She's fucking lying. Why the hell would a federal agent lie right to a cop's face?"

"Because she's hiding something she doesn't want us to know. But she's giving me access to the evidence, so that's something."

"I don't believe a word that bitch says. Something's not right here."

Emmett wasn't about to argue that point, but he wasn't sure what the hell was going on or why either. There *could* be a legitimate reason for the lies, though he couldn't think of one currently.

Maybe his mother could.

Robash might be dirty.

But why wrap up the case this way if Jeff didn't do it. If the killer were still out there, they wouldn't want someone taking the credit for their kills.

No serial killer would allow that. Their egos were too big.

"Why doesn't she want me to have the letter from my dad?" Trinity asked softly. She rested her head against the wall and closed her eyes. "Thank you for making sure I got it." She blinked her eyes open.

"You're welcome." He squeezed her forearm. "I'm going to see if my mom and maybe my lawyer brother and father can meet with us. They might have some insight into why Robash is lying, what purpose that might serve, and can help us go through some of the evidence."

"You're going to let me look at it?"

"When a cop raises you, you tend to follow the rules."

Trinity laughed.

"Only my dad is a defense attorney, so the joke was always that if one of us ever got busted, we'd have good representation."

"You're joking, right?"

"Nope." Without thinking, he laced his fingers with hers and tugged her through the lobby of the federal building. "It's one of the many reasons my parents ended up divorced. I mean, my mom arrested them, and my dad defended them. But the point is, my mom *has* told me there are times to bend the rules. I think she'd agree that this is one of them."

7

Trinity dangled her feet in the pool and stared out at the inlet. A couple of fishing vessels returned from the ocean. A few other boats floated in the water, enjoying the last few hours of daylight before the sun dipped behind the horizon.

She could get used to this.

Not that there weren't beaches and waterways up in Pensacola, because there were. Plenty of them, too.

But she didn't live on them.

Truth be told, she had only moved back to Pensacola after she and Alex had called it quits.

For good.

But she hadn't liked Atlanta. She'd only moved there because he was there. But when their relationship ended, she'd come running back to Florida with her tail between her legs.

Her cell rang.

Kathy.

Trinity contemplated not answering. Kathy had texted five times already today, asking for an update. But if Trinity didn't answer, Kathy would keep it up.

"Hi, Kath." Trinity continued kicking her legs, enjoying the warmth of the pool. "Sorry I haven't texted or called. It's been a busy day."

"Doing what? Because I've been worried about you. I almost got in my car and started driving."

Now that was dramatic. "Emmett and I went and spoke to the FBI, and then we did some research at the police station. Right now, I'm waiting for him and his mom, the chief of police."

"Why? Didn't you find out everything you needed to know from the FBI? I mean, I just watched the evening news. The district attorney's office made a statement. I'm sorry, but you need to accept—"

"Kathy, I can't." Trinity rubbed her temple. "The FBI lied. Right to my face. And to Emmett's. They're covering something up. I have to see this through."

"Okay. I'm coming to Lighthouse Cove. Give me

the address of where you're staying. See if they have another room."

"Now you're being ridiculous." Trinity glanced at the sky, angling her face toward the sun. "Don't get mad, but I don't want you to come. I'm sure I'll be back in a few days."

"Trinity, I care about you, and I'm concerned that you're looking for an answer you're never going to find." Kathy might be right, but Trinity had to at least search.

"I'll call you tomorrow night. Promise."

The sound of shoes shuffling across the stone patio caught her attention. She ended the call and glanced over her shoulder.

It was hard not to smile when she made eye contact with Emmett.

"You remember my mom, Rebecca," Emmett said. "And this is my dad, Dalton."

Trinity jumped to her feet. "It's nice to meet you." She stretched out her hand. "Thank you for coming."

"I'm sorry my son, Seth, couldn't make it," Rebecca said. "One of his kids is sick, and another one has practice, so he and his wife have to split duties."

"I appreciate the help you're giving me. Really, I do. This goes above and beyond." She followed

Emmett to the round table under the umbrella and took a seat, still facing the water. The view had a calming effect, and she needed it. While she hadn't lost her temper since she'd been in her early twenties, she'd felt heat boiling in her belly ever since they left the federal offices in Fort Lauderdale. Her therapist had told her that while she dealt with the betrayal that had sent her over the edge, she would always have to balance her emotions when pushed to her limits.

"If I didn't think something strange was going on, I'd let it go," Rebecca said. "But Robash sent me logged evidence that I know is false. I can prove it, but I don't want to show my hand too fast. Not until I know more, especially since she took over the crime scene before I even had a chance to look at anything."

"I don't mean to be rude, and I'm certainly not questioning you, but why wouldn't you be part of it since it happened in your town and Emmett was right there?"

"That's a good question. And a valid one." Rebecca leaned back in her chair. Her ex-husband sat to her right, and Emmett was on her left, closer to Trinity. "I was in my office doing paperwork when Robash and her team showed up. They said they had gotten a tip that Jeff was in the area and wanted to know if we'd seen him. Of course, no one had at the time. However, shortly after she showed up, she got an *anonymous tip* that someone had spotted him in front of the diner. That's when I radioed my son, who was with your dad. Once we had confirmation of the situation, Robash took over. It didn't matter that I'm in charge here. Once the state police and the feds rolled in, my hands were tied. It was their case, their call. I was only there to support them, but I had no reason to believe that any of them would pull shit like this."

"Before we continue,"—Dalton leaned forward, clasping his hands together. He had kind, deep blue eyes, much like Emmett—"I need you to give me a dollar so I can officially be your lawyer."

"Do I need one?" She found a bill in the bottom of her purse and handed it to Dalton. It seemed silly, but she'd do whatever was necessary to clear her father.

"This isn't about need. It's about us taking on the federal government."

Trinity rubbed her hands up and down her thighs. "All I want is for my father to have the opportunity to prove he didn't do the things he was accused of. As if he were still alive."

Emmett took her hand. "If you want to do that, you've got to challenge Robash. My mom and I are going after her regardless."

"What do you mean?" Trinity asked.

"We don't tell the public a lot of things about murder cases," Rebecca said. "We have to keep things out of the media to preserve evidence and to protect our citizens. Or to trip up the killer. But we generally don't keep those things from other law enforcement agencies. When Robash sent me the evidence that she *claims* was in the envelope, Emmett and I decided that she's making sure this case is wrapped up nice and neat and that your father goes down."

"She can't do that. It's wrong." Trinity tried to swallow, but her throat was too dry. "And what if my father didn't do it? There will be more killings. How would she explain that?" She hated doubting, for even a second, that her dad was innocent.

"I'm sorry. But, unfortunately, most of the evidence is pretty damning," Rebecca said.

"Robash destroyed the sketch, the personal note to you, and the dates and times sheet, replacing it with a more detailed version of a kill list. It made it easy for her superior to allow her to declare the Adultery Killer case officially closed," Emmett said.

"After reviewing some of what she sent over to our office, it's become painfully obvious that Robash believed they had the right guy and wanted a clean finish."

"What do you believe?" Trinity stared deeply into Emmett's eyes. She had no idea why his opinion mattered so much. Maybe it was because she felt as though no one was on her side—not even her mother since she'd tried to talk her out of coming to Lighthouse Cove to begin with. Not to mention, her parents had more doubt about her dad's innocence than she did. "Now that you've seen the evidence, done more research, do you think my dad killed all those men?" She took a short breath. "Would you have closed the case?"

"I would have honestly leaned toward your dad as being guilty, but I would have looked into the sketch. I would have continued investigating, and I sure as hell wouldn't have shot him. I would have wanted him to defend himself," Emmett said clearly and with an even tone. "Robash is ambitious, and she was getting a lot of pressure from her superiors because she'd begged for that case and wasn't making too much headway. She did have solid eyewitnesses who saw your dad with the victims. And there was physical evidence at each crime scene that belonged to your dad. But what she did to button up the case was wrong."

"I've started to look at some of the evidence, and I have questions," Dalton said. "While hair fibers and DNA were found at the crime scenes, they look staged. And when I do a deep-dive into your father, I just don't see him as an organized killer in that way."

Trinity bit back the sob that filled her throat. She stood, turned her back on the group, and hugged her middle. She hadn't known her father at all. She'd had one meeting with him when she'd been sixteen. That was it. And from that encounter, all she remembered was the rage and hatred that had darkened her soul. Not only for her father—a murderer—but at her mom and Ben for lying to her about it all.

The pain that'd filled her heart had lived inside her for years. It'd nearly destroyed her humanity.

"My dad is a two-dimensional being to me," she managed to choke out. "I didn't know he existed until he finished serving his sentence—probation and all. He'd given me up, allowing Ben to adopt me. It's odd. For most of my life, I called Ben 'Dad.' I stopped that in my late teens."

"What do you call him now?" Emmett appeared at her side, wrapping a warm, protective arm around her waist.

"Around my twenty-fifth birthday, I started calling him Dad again. He did adopt me and raise me. But we can say *Ben* so as not to confuse the issue for now." She leaned into Emmett's strength. After she'd found out about her biological father, she'd sworn that she'd never rely on another person again. Having the two people who were supposed to love and take care of her betray her, had destroyed her innocence.

But then Alex had come into her life. He'd washed away all her defenses. Made her want to be a better person. She used to think she'd been able to mend her relationships with her mom and Ben because of Alex, but she knew now that wasn't entirely true. She and her parents had worked hard in therapy to make that happen.

And she'd spent time in anger management classes.

That had nothing to do with Alex.

She'd completely given him her heart without reservation, and he'd taken it and run. The worst part was that when he was done, he'd neglected to tell her until *after* he'd already moved on.

That hurt.

A lot.

She'd not only trusted him with her soul, but she'd also trusted him with her loyalty.

Taking in a deep breath, she broke the skin-to-skin contact with Emmett. A coolness trickled across her body as if a cold front had come down from the north.

Emmett narrowed his stare but respectfully followed her lead and made his way back to the table, taking a seat next to his mother.

Emmett and his family and friends could help her find answers.

But she wouldn't rely on him for anything else. All that had to come from within. The only person she could completely count on was herself. That was a lesson she'd learned the hard way one too many times.

"This isn't my place, but I've got a little experience in this department." Dalton pushed to a standing position. "Both Ben and Jeff are your father in different ways. One is biological, and the other is in every way that counts."

"That's not entirely fair," Rebecca said with some animosity.

"I wasn't finished." Dalton stepped in front of Trinity and placed both of his hands on her biceps. "I raised a child that wasn't biologically mine, and while I was pretty sure of that fact when I made the decision to do it, he's still my boy, even though his dad is back in the picture. No one can ever take that away from me, just like I can't take the biology away from Steve. All that said, the two relationships are very different, and I feel bad for you that you never got the chance to know your biological father."

She chuckled. She didn't mean to, but it came out. "He killed someone."

"I know. I read the transcript of his plea deal and his prison and parole reports. He made a mistake and paid a huge price for it." Dalton pursed his lips. "I'm not sure I believe that he murdered sixteen more men. If he were my client, I'd be focusing on this sketch he made—and damn, he was talented."

"I had no idea he could do that." Her heart broke into a million pieces. Her father, Jeff, had chosen to give her up and let Ben adopt her. She was grateful for that. Ben had always been by her side, especially through the tough years. He'd taken the brunt of her anger and did so because he'd chosen to love her. He didn't have to. She turned and faced Emmett and his mother. "Can I ask the two of you a question? And will you be totally honest?"

"Of course," Emmett said. "I won't lie to you."

"Neither will I." Rebecca nodded.

"If you believe my dad could be guilty, then why are we all here doing this?"

"As cops, we deal in facts and evidence," Rebecca said. "There was enough evidence to arrest your father—which is what we would have done given the chance."

"I would have stepped in and offered to defend him." Dalton squeezed her shoulder. "There are too many questions that don't have answers that fit neatly."

"This is one of the few times where my ex-husband and I work well together." Rebecca smiled. "The system is flawed."

"Not to mention the corruption that exists," Dalton said under his breath.

"Let's not start on that argument." Rebecca shook her head. "Because I can rattle off ten crooked lawyers off the top of my head."

Dalton held up his hands and laughed. "Fair enough."

Trinity rubbed her temples. "So, what do we do next? Because I feel like there is no hope of clearing my father's name. Or…what is the point? He's a homeless guy. Who cares?" She shook her head.

"We care," Emmett said. "It's why we're sitting here with you right now."

"Even if he did do it. We can't have people like Robash swapping out real evidence with doctored information that we don't even know is real." Dalton tapped the files on the table. "Something bigger is going on here. I think we can all agree on that."

"We can," Rebecca said. "But what? Robash would have to be quite certain that Jeff was the killer. Because if he wasn't, and more bodies started piling up, that would destroy her career."

"So, what does she know that we don't?" Emmett asked.

Trinity slumped into the chair, tears burning the corners of her eyes. "He must have done it."

"Hey," Emmett whispered. "We don't know that, and we're going to re-examine all the evidence."

"We're going to go over all the crime scenes," Dalton said. "And I'm going to have my team talk to witnesses and treat this as if I were going to defend it in a court of law."

"We'll get the answers you need," Emmett said.

"Why?" Trinity lifted her gaze, catching Emmett's attention. "Why are you doing this for me?"

"It's not just for you." He took her hand. "Your father asked me to do something right before he was killed. I owe it to him."

"I don't like it when other law enforcement

agencies fuck with me, my department, and especially my kids," Rebecca said. "But I especially take it personally when a case isn't wrapped up neatly on my watch. I can't let this go. People died. It's my job to protect the citizens of Lighthouse Cove. No offense, but it's not only about you; it's about everyone this case has touched."

"As for me," Dalton said, "everyone deserves a good defense. And everyone is innocent until proven guilty. Period."

"I don't know how to thank you." Trinity squared her shoulders. Ben would likely remind her that tears didn't make her weak; they only served to remind her that she was human. That she had emotions other than rage and that it could only be seen as a good thing.

Dalton glanced at his wrist. "It's getting late. I'd better get going. I'll be in touch in the morning."

"Thanks, Dad." Emmett reached his arm across the table.

"I'll walk out with your father." Rebecca leaned in and kissed Emmett's cheek. "Talk to you tomorrow."

Trinity waited for Emmett to follow his parents, but he didn't. Instead, he sat on the pool patio, staring into her eyes with kindness and understanding.

He had a sweet soul, and she found herself wanting to lose herself in his arms. No. It was more than desire. It was a need that she felt in every muscle. It took over every thought. She couldn't shake it.

But she needed to.

Suddenly, he took her chin with his thumb and forefinger. Her breath caught. His warm mouth brushed over hers in a hot kiss, sensation exploding across her lips in a fiery blaze. Her toes curled as she gripped his shoulders.

It had been a long time since a man had made her feel as if she were the center of the universe.

She pressed her hand to the center of his chest. "I'm sorry," she whispered.

"For what?"

"I can't do this." The urge to race off to her room was almost unbearable, but she resisted. She held her ground and decided she would speak her truth. "You're a good man, and I like you. Maybe if—"

He pressed his finger over her lips. "No need to say anything else. I shouldn't have done that." He stood.

"I don't mean to hurt you."

"You haven't." He smiled. "Melinda's in the kitchen if you need anything, and I'm a text away."

He took her hand and kissed it. "I'll see you tomorrow." With that, he turned on his heels and strolled across the patio and into the house as if he hadn't a care in the world.

She groaned.

Emmett was one of a kind, and as the heat from his lips dissipated, a pang of regret filled her heart.

8

Trinity took her bagel and her cup of coffee out to the dock. She had no desire to hang out with the other guests and make small talk. Besides, the morning headline had been all about her father, and the first thing she'd heard from someone staying at the bed and breakfast was how the world was a safer place because the police had taken out "that murdering bastard."

Trinity didn't need to hear that kind of talk.

Especially after her sleepless night.

She settled in at the end, dangling her feet in the salty water.

She took a big bite of her bagel with cream cheese piled on a quarter of an inch thick. "Oh, that's good," she whispered. She focused on her exploding taste buds and did her best to ignore the lingering thoughts of Emmett that had filled her mind. She didn't know what bothered her more.

The fact that the dreams were the only things that had gotten her through the night.

Or that she'd tried to relive them the second she blinked open her eyes.

She touched her lips.

His kiss had only lasted a minute, but she'd never forget the feel of his mouth pressed firmly to hers or how it'd made her head spin. It was as if she'd been kissed for the very first time.

The wood planks under her ass vibrated.

She glanced over her shoulder.

Melinda.

"There you are." Melinda scurried down the dock with her tall mug. "Did you get enough to eat? My staff said you didn't request a hot breakfast either morning."

Trinity raised her bagel. "Plenty. Thank you."

"Emmett called me and wanted to make sure you were getting special treatment." Melinda plopped down on the dock and sat cross-legged. "As if I wouldn't make sure my guests had everything they needed." Melinda tilted her head toward the sun. "He asked if you'd seen the newspaper. I told him I had no idea because that's the truth. But I'm wondering if maybe you haven't answered a text or a message. I know. None of my business."

"I've seen it," Trinity said matter-of-factly. "And I'm ignoring my phone in general right now." Mostly, she didn't want to deal with Kathy, who'd started in at six this morning.

"Emmett's a good man. One of the best. And while he and I weren't meant for each other, I still care a great deal about him and would do pretty much anything for him—including this little errand."

Trinity swallowed the thick lump that formed in her throat. Here came the harsh words of judgment. Ever since Jeff Allen had become a person of interest and then the prime suspect in the Adultery Killer case, Trinity had gotten used to people looking at her with fear and hatred.

Of course, she'd learned to live with those judgmental glances when she turned sixteen and not only found out who her biological father was, but her friends and their parents did, as well.

"When you first got here, I had no idea who you were. I honestly thought you might be someone from one of his brothers' pasts, or maybe a long-lost family member. Another half-sibling or something like that. However, I put things together pretty quickly the first night. I'm sure others did, too."

"I can be out of your hair in an hour," Trinity said.

Melinda jerked her head back. "I'm not asking you to leave. Though I will ask that you continue keeping your identity from my guests—I don't need them checking out. But I don't think it's fair for you to be judged for what your father may or may not have done."

"I appreciate that." Trinity's heart lurched. Normally, when people found out who her father was, even before this latest scandal, they all looked at her a little strangely. Most told her it didn't bother them, but they all slowly distanced themselves as the days and weeks passed. "I don't want to cause you any problems. I know you need a certain number of people to keep this place running."

"You let me worry about my business." Melinda lowered her chin and arched a brow. "Emmett is very good at what he does. If your father didn't do what he was accused of, Emmett will prove it."

"That sounds strange, considering he's a cop."

"It wouldn't be the first time he's proven something like that." Melinda set her coffee aside.

"We hooked up because he had to arrest me when my grandfather was murdered."

"Excuse me?" Trinity coughed as she nearly choked on a small piece of bagel. She washed it down with some hot and bitter brew. "I'm so sorry."

"It was hell, and the worst part was that my own father set me up."

Trinity stuck her finger in her ear. "I'm sorry. What?"

"You heard correctly." Melinda pointed to the big white house on the water. "It was all over that place and what to do with it. My grandfather wanted to preserve it, and my father wanted to sell it. He was tired of dealing with it. My mom loved the idea of turning it into a bed and breakfast and sharing it with everyone. My grandfather owned it, and to piss off my father, he cut him out of the will and left it to me, knowing I'd side with my mom."

"How did he know that?"

"I went to school for hotel management and hospitality. This is my jam. I love it."

"You're really good at it, too," Trinity said.

"Thank you." Melinda's gaze wandered toward the inlet. "To make a very long story a little shorter, my father, the crazy bastard, decided to kill his father-in-law and make it look like I did it so I wouldn't get the Landon Lighthouse Bed and Breakfast. It was Emmett who proved I didn't do it. Even though he was the one who found enough evidence to arrest me." Melinda rubbed her wrists. "Ruined being tied up as a sexy thing forever."

Trinity laughed. "No way in hell would I ever let someone tie me up. However, I might be inclined to do the tying."

"I hear you on that, sister." Melinda raised her coffee and took a sip. "I'm going to give you an unsolicited piece of advice for dealing with some people from this town."

"Okay."

"For the most part, everyone is super cool, but some will point their fingers, walk on the other side of the road, and call you names. I still have some who won't stay here because of what happened, and then others who come just because of what my father did. Thing is, I hold my head up and pretend I don't give a shit. I act like the same spoiled girl who complained about the stuff that didn't go my way or wasn't like I thought it should be." She leaned a little closer. "The people of this town don't know you, but don't give them a reason to dislike you."

"Are you implying I'm behaving like a bitch or something?" Trinity's mouth went dry. Heat filled her veins. All those old anger triggers flashed in her mind.

"No. But you are elusive and a bit unapproachable. People here don't know what to make of you, and that gives them something to talk and wonder about. Made even more so by the fact that you're hanging out with Emmett and the portion of his family who are cops and lawyers. That's the last thing you want when you're trying to keep your association to someone hidden."

Trinity had to admit that Melinda had a valid point. In trying to blend into the scenery, Trinity had managed to make herself even more noticeable. But she didn't want to make friends, either.

Melinda gently placed her hand on Trinity's knee. "I would hate for people to treat you badly because of your dad. You did nothing wrong regardless of what he did or didn't do. It has nothing to do with you."

"You have no idea what that means to me."

Melinda smiled. "I kind of do."

"Yeah. I guess you do." Trinity laughed.

"On to topic number two." Melinda held up two of her fingers. "What's going on between you and my ex—and don't try to tell me nothing, because I know him, and I know when he's got the hots for someone."

Heat filled Trinity's cheeks like a marshmallow catching fire when shoved into the flames. "We just met."

"Emmett hasn't had a relationship since we broke up. Not one that's worth mentioning anyway. Sure, he's dated, but nothing serious. And when he fell for me, it was about the time he slapped on the second handcuff—which was funny because we'd known each other for our entire lives, and he'd never paid me any attention until I became a murder suspect."

"I'm no psychology major, but if your assessment is true, then Emmett has issues." Trinity tucked her hair behind her ears and lowered her gaze, hoping her face hadn't turned bright red.

"I don't know about that. Still, when he falls in love, he falls fast and hard," Melinda said. "Before me, it was with his high school sweetheart of nearly five years. Everyone thought they would get married, but he never asked. After that, he was with a woman who wasn't from around here for a couple of years, but that relationship was destined to fail because she wanted nothing to do with Lighthouse Cove, and there's no getting Emmett to leave. No one in that family is leaving, and I can't blame them."

"This is an amazing little town. I feel like I'm in my own little safe harbor."

"Ah. So, you'd stay if the circumstances were right?" Melinda winked.

Trinity touched her lips. That kiss had been all she'd thought about since it'd happened. She wouldn't mind getting to know Emmett better, but not while all this stuff with her father was going on. That would only complicate things. And after everything that'd happened with Alex, complicated wasn't something she was willing to do again.

"I'm sorry. I shouldn't be giving you shit about Emmett," Melinda said. "Only, I can tell he has a crush on you."

"He is incredibly sexy and has such kind eyes. I don't think I've ever met a man where I could see right into their soul before."

"That's Emmett." Melinda turned, dropping her feet into the water. "But don't ever mistake that kindness for weakness. He might have a heart of gold, but if you cross him or hurt any of his family, he'll come at you like a bull seeing red."

"I can tell that about him. And his mother."

"Oh. Rebecca. She's an interesting character." Melinda kicked her feet, making a swirling motion. "But all of them are good people."

"Do you mind if I ask why you and Emmett didn't work out?" Trinity's heart jumped around in her chest like a jackhammer. She shouldn't be prying into other people's business.

Especially Emmett's.

"We tell people a lot of things. Like that Emmett is totally dedicated to his career and won't retire anytime soon. He will protect and serve until someone tells him he's not capable, but he won't go away quietly. I loved that about him. However, I always wished he didn't work as much as he did, and that sometimes became an issue for us."

"He is passionate about his job. That's not a bad thing. My ex hated my schedule as a nurse."

"Long, odd hours can be rough on a relationship." Melinda nodded. "And then there were our other reasons. They're private, and I won't get into those except to say that it's not bad or any reason that someone shouldn't get involved with Emmett. He's a good man. As I said, one of the best. We just couldn't be together."

"Kind of sounds like me and my ex, only he ended up being a shit."

"Okay. You have to explain that one," Melinda said. "Because Emmett was never an asshole. Not even when things got bad."

Trinity leaned back and angled her face so she got the maximum amount of sun. She closed her eyes and let all the memories flood her brain, but she tried not to let the emotions hit her too hard. She couldn't afford to feel them. Not right now anyway.

"Alex and I met when he was visiting a buddy of his from college. There was instant chemistry between us, and we began a long-distance relationship immediately. After three months, I found a job in Atlanta and moved."

"What kind of nurse are you?"

"I work in the ER."

"That's a commendable career."

"I love it." Trinity nodded. "Anyway. I moved in with Alex, and things were perfect. We were madly in love—until I got pregnant."

Melinda gasped and placed her hand over her belly. "He didn't want kids?"

"He wanted them. So, we were happy. But I had some complications around the sixth month and went into labor. During the delivery, I started to hemorrhage. The doctors did everything they could, but not only did we lose our child, I ended up having to get an emergency hysterectomy." Trinity swiped at the tears that burned a path down her cheeks. It had been a while since she'd told this story, and for some reason, it felt good to purge the emotions. The last time she'd relayed this information, her heart had turned black as if someone had reached into the cavity of her chest and cut off the blood supply.

"I'm so sorry." Melinda scooted closer and hugged her tightly. "That's fucking horrible."

That had to be the best response anyone had ever given her. Usually, people pitied her or stared at her with a blank look and couldn't even manage anything other than a *sorry*, if that.

"I can't even imagine what that must have been like for you," Melinda said.

"It was horrible," Trinity admitted. "It wasn't just losing our baby, but the idea that I'd never be able to have a child. That's what destroyed our relationship."

"Emmett is going to kill me for this one, but we can relate."

Trinity's gaze dipped to Melinda's midriff. "You can't have children?" she whispered.

"My husband and I are doing IVF. We just did our first round. I'm freaking out that I could be pregnant, but he's gone, so I'm waiting to find out. I'm almost forty, so the older I get, the harder it will be. However, I'm getting sidetracked." She blew out a puff of air. "I'm just going to say it... Emmett can't father a child, but he didn't want to spend the money on fertility treatments and all that. He just wanted to adopt, and I wanted to try to have a baby the natural way. I became so desperate to have a child that I pushed him right out the door."

"Not being able to give someone something they want can change a person." Trinity's heart went out to both Melinda and Emmett, but she could especially relate to him. "Alex and I struggled. Not only were we grieving the loss of our child, but he never looked at me the same way after the hysterectomy. Less than a year later, I found out that he was having an affair. He's married now with a kid on the way."

"Oh. Wow. That has to hurt something awful." Melinda's face contorted as if she'd eaten sour candy. It was like someone had given her a little jab to the gut.

"I'm sorry if that hit a little too close to home," Trinity said. "It's not the same thing."

"No. I never cheated on Emmett. Nor did he on me. But I have to say, hearing it shows me how selfish I was—how selfish I *am*."

Trinity took Melinda's hand. "Wanting to have a child that grows inside you is not self-centered. I don't know how either of you processed his inability to have kids. I can only tell you that Alex didn't take it well with me. He was angry and wanted to sue the hospital for negligence. He was more upset that I lost my uterus than a child. It was more about the potential of life than life itself for him."

"That's harsh."

"I know." Trinity allowed the flood of despair that mixed with the deep-seated lurking darkness of her soul to come to the surface. But every once in a while, they had to rise, and this felt like a safe place to do it. "I often wonder what kind of father he'll make. Will the child be a whole person to him, or will he live vicariously through his kid? Looking back on my life with Alex, while he was kind and decent, he wasn't as loving as I thought he was. He went through the motions, but it was all superficial. I'm not sure he understands what true love is."

"That's sad, especially when I can see how deeply you loved him."

"I did." There was no denying how much she'd cared for Alex. She'd given him her entire being, and he'd taken it without giving much back.

She only had herself to blame.

Never again.

Sucking in a deep breath, she let it out slowly, ridding herself of the toxic memories, holding onto only the thoughts and emotions her therapist reminded her she needed to keep in her heart. "That part of my life is in the past. I'm working on building a future, and I know I'll find someone to share my life with."

Melinda's eyes twinkled like the stars dancing in the night sky.

"Don't even go there," Trinity said.

"Go where?" Melinda asked with a tilt of her head and a wink. "You and Emmett would make such a cute couple."

"I live in Pensacola." Trinity held up her hand. "I'm only here to clear my father's name, and Emmett was the last person to see him alive. He's not even interested in me."

"*Right*. Next thing you're going to tell me is that he didn't kiss you last night."

"Are you spying on your guests?"

Melinda laughed. "I was cleaning up in the kitchen. It was hard to miss."

"Anyone ever tell you that's called burying the lead?" This was the kind of thing that would normally upset Trinity. She hated being blindsided, and there was nothing worse than people getting all up in her business. She enjoyed her privacy, especially after losing her baby. That had been absolutely horrible. Worse than when everyone had found out that her father was a murderer. With the latter, people made assumptions. Their judgments were harsh and cold, but they were done to her face.

With the former, her friends and even some of her family pitied her and talked about her behind her back as if she were a fragile little girl who couldn't handle the big, bad world.

"I drive Chad insane with that. He'll come home from a business trip and ask me how things are going, and I'll tell him all the superficial stuff and then drop the bomb. He hates it."

"I would, too."

"And now you're changing the subject."

Trinity laughed as she hopped to her feet, thankful to see Emmett waving from the pool deck. Standing next to him were two incredibly handsome men. "Who are the two guys with Emmett?"

Melinda slowly stood, covering her eyes. "One is Rhett, the private eye. And the other is Emmerson. He's another cop."

"Jesus. That family produces some handsome guys."

"And they are all so disgustingly sweet."

"I've met Jamison and his wife. Are Rhett and Emmerson married?"

"Rhett is a confirmed bachelor. He's always

bringing the flavor of the month around. Emmerson isn't currently single but he's also not married. He's been on and off with this fishing charter captain. Nice woman, but they are like oil and water."

"Sometimes, that makes for the best relationships."

"But you know what?" Melinda looped her hand through Trinity's arm. "You have to get to know a person for more than a single kiss to find out if your oil is suited for someone else's water."

"That makes no sense at all." Trinity's stomach flipped. And flopped. And sloshed around like she was a teenager about to go meet a boy under the bleachers.

"I'll bet you the full price of your stay at my lovely bed and breakfast that you and Emmett end up in bed together before my husband comes home from his business trip."

"Never going to happen," Trinity said. "When does Chad return?"

"Five days."

Trinity swallowed her pulse. She could hold out that long. It wouldn't be *that* hard to resist his charms.

Then he smiled, and all she wanted to do was pick up where they'd left off last night.

9

*E*mmett held the SUV's door and helped Trinity into the front seat.

"Where are we going?"

"To the park by the beach," Emmett said. "Emmerson and I were starting to make people uncomfortable at the bed and breakfast. The last thing we need is to draw attention to you, and if the police are visiting you all the time, it's going to make people wonder."

"Melinda mentioned that I should be more social when I'm there. Maybe talk to some people. Outside of work, I'm generally pretty introverted."

Emmett shut the door and raced around the hood of his vehicle. He slid behind the steering wheel and turned the key. He loved the sound of a V-8 turning over and couldn't resist revving it a bit. Childish, but he didn't care.

She glanced in his direction with an arched brow.

He shrugged. "I don't even know what you do for a living."

"I'm an ER nurse."

"Nice," he said. "That's a hard but rewarding career."

"I love it. Most of my friends end up leaving the ER for something a bit tamer, but I can't imagine doing anything else." She pressed her hands over her stomach. Quickly, she ran her hands down her thighs. "Unless I had a family, but I'm not sure that's ever going to happen."

"Why not?"

"First off, I'm thirty-six, and I'm not getting any younger. I have no boyfriend to speak of and no prospects. Besides, my life is complicated. It would be asking a lot of someone to be a part of it."

Emmett drove the mile down the road from the bed and breakfast and into the parking lot. "Because of your father?" His family dynamic was insanely cumbersome. To most, it looked like a nighttime soap opera, but to him and the rest of his siblings, it was just life. However, his world had taken a sharp left turn when he found out that children wouldn't come naturally to him. But it got worse when Melinda became adamant that they spend a ridiculous amount of money on something that might not work when there were kids out there who needed to be loved.

He thought about adopting a child by himself at times, but that might be hard at forty and as a cop.

"That's one reason," she said. "The other is something I don't like to talk about much."

"No pressure from me." He pushed the gearshift into park and turned to face Trinity. He hadn't been able to get her out of his mind since he'd met her, and it was making him crazy. Not in a bad way, but it was a distraction, and he didn't want it to affect the work he was doing to help clear her father's name.

Or at least get answers.

He still wasn't sure what he believed.

Or didn't believe.

Except that Robash was a fucking liar. That much was for damn sure. And Rhett had something to dish on Cotania, but he wanted Trinity present. Emmett could only hope that whatever it was, it was good news and not more feds and cops doing bad shit. He hated that.

Of course, turning all this over in his head was the only way he got that damn kiss off his brain.

"You and Melinda seem to have a decent enough relationship, considering you were engaged at one point," Trinity said. "Do you like her husband?"

"Chad? He's a great guy." Emmett shifted in his seat. Melinda, while she was a great host and usually knew when to stay out of her guests' way, didn't always know when to do that with her friends. "Why do you ask?"

"I don't know. You both seem a little overprotective of each other in a weird way."

He chuckled. "We can be. I only want the best for her. That said, I know her, and I know how she can get. So, I sometimes feel for Chad, and that pisses her off. She thinks I take his side in things." He held up his finger, pressing it over Trinity's lips when she opened her mouth. "Chad is good friends with my eldest brother. I've known him forever. But, truth be told, he used to hate me."

"Why?"

"Because of Melinda. He liked her back in the day and always thought I stole her away. They hadn't even gone on a date when I had to arrest her."

"She told me all about that."

Emmett swallowed his breath. "What else did she tell you?" Melinda hadn't broken his trust too many times, but he could see her doing it with Trinity, especially after the teasing text she'd sent him last night about the kiss she'd witnessed.

Not that his infertility was a joking matter, but ever since Melinda had gotten married, she'd made it her life's mission to find Emmett a woman.

"Only that—"

Tap. Tap.

Rhett banged on the window.

She gasped.

He jerked. "Guess we'd better get out of this car and find out what Rhett learned while he was in Miami and what Emmerson has to report."

The warm, salty air hit his face as the ocean breeze kicked in. He pressed his hand against the small of Trinity's back and guided her to an empty picnic table where Emmerson had already made himself comfortable.

"It's so pretty here." Trinity climbed up onto the table and tilted her nose to the sky. "I've lived in North Florida for most of my life, and I love it there, but nothing is as spectacular as this."

"We like it." Rhett straddled the bench. "Not to be rude, but I have three other cases I'm working."

"And with Mom and Emmett both taking a personal day, I'm busy as hell," Emmerson said. "So, let's get this party started."

Rhett set a folder on the table and tapped it with his fingers. "Cotania was blindsided by Robash's request to take over the case. He was all set to work jointly with the Fort Lauderdale office when she found tiny discrepancies in his evidence collection for three of the cases." Rhett opened the folder. "And not even anything that would hurt the case. But here's the thing. The evidence points away from Jeff Allen."

"Where *does* it point?" Trinity yanked the piece of paper closer and held it up. "What am I looking at?"

"First things first," Rhett said. "There was no note with the first three kills. But all three men *were* cheating on their wives. They were all brutally murdered with a knife. But the pattern was slightly different, though Cotania thinks they were the same guy based on the cuts to the neck. Every victim has the same slash on the left side of their necks under the ear and down to the throat. That doesn't change."

"All that tells me is that our killer decided his

message wasn't loud enough to be heard," Emmett said.

"Agreed." Rhett nodded. "But here is where it gets really interesting." Rhett licked his fingers, thumbed through a couple of pieces of paper, and then handed Emmett a report. "Trinity is holding the reports from the three murders before the notes started showing up on the victims. What I just gave you are murders that have no notes but are similar. And they happened *after* Jeff Allen migrated to Fort Lauderdale."

"Are you saying you have proof that our killer is still out there?" Emmerson asked as he leaned over Emmett's shoulder.

"Not proof. But a working theory." Rhett ran a hand over the top of his head. "Cotania has a man in custody who claims he killed these six men. He's given them enough details they didn't release to the media that even Cotania's boss is listening. But that still leaves a lot of other dead bodies that Jeff could be responsible for."

"All with a note pinned to them with Paul's name on it. But there's more," Rhett said. "Cotania shared with me that he believes Robash not only lied to get the case but that she also sabotaged him."

"How?" Emmerson asked.

"It's all in that folder. But to summarize, she formally accused him of sexual harassment."

"When the fuck did she do that?" Emmett asked.

"Three months before they officially assigned her the case. But she was already working it, at least from what I can tell," Rhett said. "There was no basis for the charges, but it's a stain on Cotania's record."

"We have to believe the victim," Emmerson said. "If she said he did something, even if she's a lying sack of shit, he might have made her feel uncomfortable somehow."

"All agreed," Rhett said. "However, witnesses signed statements that what she said happened, didn't." Rhett held up a finger. "They were all women. All who stated that Robash would do anything to get ahead." He looked between the three of them. "This woman is not well-liked."

"She's why victim-shaming exists," Trinity mumbled under her breath. "But we still always have to listen."

"That's the truth of the matter." Emmett would always take the word of a potential victim. As an officer of the law, he had to. If the world were to change, it was his duty as a man who generally had the power to ensure it.

However, Trinity was right. Robash muddied the

waters. When someone like Robash, a woman in power, took advantage of her position, all it did was make it even harder to make progress.

"But you all have to understand that while Cotania can't stand Robash and would love to see her fail, he *does* believe Jeff is guilty of some of these murders. He just thinks Robash wanted insurance, so she doctored a few things."

"That's illegal." Trinity tossed the paper across the table. "No offense, but you wonder why so many people don't trust the cops."

"I don't ponder that." Rhett chuckled. "I've sent copies of all of this to Mom, Dad, Seth, and all of you. I'll keep digging, as well. "

"Do you want to know what doesn't make sense to me?" Trinity jumped off the table and twisted her back. "My dad left Pensacola when I was sixteen, seven years after he was released from prison. Why were there no murders in that city?"

"Funny you should mention that." Rhett waggled his finger. "For starters, he was on parole, living in a halfway house for those seven years. They monitored his every move. It might have been hard for him to commit that kind of crime without getting caught. However, I've asked for a list of all homicides even remotely similar to these, both solved and unsolved, within a hundred-mile radius." He tapped the folder.

"Okay. Then what about the eighteen years from the time he left until two years ago when these started? Because don't serial killers have to kill?" she asked.

"I've spoken to an expert on serial killers," Emmett said. "There are triggers that could cause someone to go on a rampage like this."

"Explain it to me," she said with her hands on her hips and fire shooting from her eyes.

"I don't have a full report, but the short answer is that he didn't start off as a serial killer. Something happened," Emmett said. "Perhaps he became involved with another woman who cheated. Or he saw something that triggered that memory. Or drugs. Or any number of things that could have set this in motion." Emmett inched closer, wrapping an arm around Trinity. "I know this isn't what you want to hear, but your father lived under the radar for years. We don't have a good handle on who he was or how he lived. We're trying to do that. We have contacts in the homeless community asking questions about him, trying to paint a picture, but it's going to take time."

"I have no idea who my father was." She rubbed

her temples. "And yet I know in my heart of hearts that he didn't do this."

"We're going to find the truth, one way or another," Emmett said. "I won't rest until we do. I promise." And he meant it. When he caught her gaze, it sucker punched him right in the gut.

"I'm going to keep doing deep-dives on Robash and Cotania," Rhett said.

"I've got to get back on patrol," Emmerson chimed in. "However, I'll officially request certain reports. I've found two unsolved deaths in our county in the last twenty years. They aren't close matches, but close enough that I can bullshit my way through pretending I want to see if I can attach them to your father."

"I don't want more deaths associated with him," Trinity said as the oxygen in her lungs flew out like a seagull diving into the salty water for a tasty fish.

"That's not what I'm trying to do," Emmerson attempted to reassure her, but Emmett knew he wasn't doing that great of a job based on how she scrunched her nose.

"The more we can keep Robash on the hook, the more likely it is we can get her to trip up. And if we can get her office to open an investigation into how she handled your father's case, then we can poke deeper holes into it and maybe find the real killer." Emmett ran a hand up and down her back, giving her neck a good squeeze every once in a while.

"You believe he was innocent?" Her dark lashes lowered over her blue eyes. It mesmerized him, holding him captive.

He couldn't tear his gaze away if he tried. She carried a deep sense of sadness and loss in those blue pools, and he wanted to ease that pain for her and protect her from any future sorrow. She deserved to know the truth, even if it wasn't what she wanted to hear. She needed those answers, and he wanted to be the one to give them to her.

"You all do?" she asked as if she couldn't believe that any of them were on her side.

"Please don't take this the wrong way, but this isn't about guilt or innocence right now. This is about justice and due diligence, and they didn't give your dad a fair shake," Emmett said.

"I know he didn't do this," she pleaded with him. "I get that I sound like a broken record and have no real evidence, and I've only met my father once, but something deep in my core is telling me that the feds have this all wrong. I wish I had reached out to him when the PI I hired had found him."

"What exactly did he find? Did he leave you with paperwork? Pictures?" Rhett asked.

She nodded. "I didn't use the information. I guess I only wanted to know he was alive."

"You should have told me this sooner," Emmett said softly, reining in his frustration. On the surface, there wasn't a reason for her to tell him, but the devil was in the details, and he couldn't let anything fall through the cracks.

"Can I have the name of the man you hired? I'd like to speak to him," Rhett said.

"Of course." She nodded.

"I need you to trust me. I need you to tell me everything going forward. Can you do that?" Emmett palmed her cheek, totally forgetting about his brothers. Forgetting about his surroundings. He put all his focus and energy on Trinity. "If I'm going to help you, we can't have any secrets between us. Not one. Okay?"

She curled her fingers around his wrist. "Why are you so willing to help me? You met him for what? Less than half an hour, and it was your people—"

He brushed his lips tenderly across hers in a short kiss. "Because when I looked into your father's eyes, I saw a man who wanted his daughter to know the truth. And so do I."

"I've really got to run," his brother Emmerson said, slapping him on the back.

Emmett closed his eyes for a brief moment. He always had bad timing when it came to kissing women. "See you later."

"Have a good one." Rhett waved as he took off toward the parking lot. Laughing.

Emmett tucked the folder under his arm. "Sorry." He took her hand and tugged her toward his vehicle. "I probably shouldn't have done that."

"Probably not."

"It was an intense moment." He let out a slow breath. "If you haven't noticed, I like you, and I'm finding it difficult to separate work from my attraction."

"Is that always a problem for you?"

"No." He paused in front of his vehicle. "With the exception of Melinda."

"Are you always so honest?"

"Mostly," he admitted. "I don't see the point in lying or even sugarcoating things. However, I've been told that it's not always a good approach when it comes to my dating life."

"I appreciate the way you are. But when this is over, I'm going back to Pensacola, and you're staying here. Not to mention, physical attraction doesn't make for anything."

"It's where it all begins. Besides, it's not only your looks that interest me." He lifted her hand and kissed the back of it. "Shall we go dig through a bunch of paperwork? I promise I can keep my hands to myself."

"It's your lips I'm worried about."

He chuckled. "I'll work on it."

10

Trinity pushed the laptop aside and dropped her head to the table. It landed with a thud. She groaned. "I feel like a hamster on a wheel." They'd been at Emmett's house for the last few hours going through file after file. Case after case. She wasn't sure she completely understood half the things she'd read. They'd received paperwork from homeless shelters, social workers, the private investigator she'd hired, police reports…among other things. Her eyes blurred, and her muscles ached.

Strong hands came down on her shoulders, massaging like a master. She had half a mind to shrug them off, but it felt too damn good.

She took in a slow breath and lifted her head. A full, stocked bar separated the kitchen from the dining room but it opened to the family room. Trinity had to wonder if Melinda had had something to do with the decorations in the house. It had that same beachy feel that the bed and breakfast did. Or maybe they just had similar tastes.

Emmett had gotten under her skin like thick cream moisturizer that soothed away the dryness. He made her feel like, no matter what, everything would be okay. With every brick wall they hit, he managed to fill the glass so it seemed half-full.

"According to the records all these homeless shelters sent over, my dad wasn't a bad person," she managed. "They say he was kind. That he was always trying to find work but struggled to find anything but odd jobs."

"Having to put down that you're a convicted felon on a job application doesn't make it easy for anyone to want to hire you."

"No. It doesn't." She sat up straight. "I was such a little bitch at sixteen." She shook her head. "I told my own father to fuck off and die."

"You were a kid who'd just found out that your biological father was a murderer." Emmett rested his hand on her thigh. "When Jamison learned that

Steve was his biological dad, he went nuts. And he was a grown-ass man at the time. He held a grudge for almost two years. So, don't beat yourself up over this."

"My father didn't deserve the things I said to him."

"The more you look at it that way, the more you're going to make yourself crazy." He tapped his finger on her knee. "Your father wanted you to know that he thought about you every day. You read the note. He loved you and wanted only good things for you. I don't believe for one second that he harbored any ill will."

She inhaled sharply and let it out with a big puff. "So why give me the sketch? Why did he think I would want that?"

"I'm not sure that was necessarily meant for you. He wanted me to see what was inside that envelope, and he wanted someone to continue searching for clues, which is what we're doing."

"Okay, but you basically said he gave up. He walked out of that diner, knowing they were going to kill him. Why would he do that?" So many questions continued to swirl in her brain, and the second one got answered, ten more popped up.

"I have two guesses for that." Emmett turned her

chair and leaned closer. "My mom has asked for the autopsy report. We should have it in a day or two."

She narrowed her stare. "Why would you need that?"

"Maybe he was sick. Cancer or something."

Covering her mouth, she gasped. "Why wouldn't he go seek treatment?"

"No job. No insurance. It was terminal. Who knows? But that could have been his way out."

She dropped her hand to her lap. "That's terrible."

He tilted her chin with his thumb and forefinger. "That's only one theory. My second one is two-fold. He knew he was being set up and didn't think there was a way out because he believed it was coming from one of the good guys."

"But you didn't think Robash believed she got the wrong guy."

Emmett leaned back. "I don't know anymore. She might be a pawn, or she might be a player, but some of this stuff that Rhett got from Cotania makes me think something bigger is going on." He reached across the table and shuffled through some of the paperwork they'd spread across the surface. "According to Cotania, Robash called him numerous times regarding the case, and each time she all but told him he had it wrong. She had her team working the case when she was told it was off-limits. When her boss questioned her about it, she told him—no, she *showed* him—proof that an informant had been reaching out to her, but she wouldn't reveal her source. Still won't." Emmett tapped a piece of paper. "We need to find whoever she was working with."

"I have to assume you've asked."

"Of course, but she's doing exactly what I'd do and protecting her sources. She has to. Otherwise, he or she will never come forward again. But what fascinates me is that Robash asked for the files to the first few murders that didn't have the notes with Paul's name on them *before* she started making a pest of herself."

"Why does that matter?"

"Because the more I study those crime scenes, the more they don't match up. Or should I say the more the latter ones look staged to look like the first ones."

"My head hurts." Trinity stood and made her way toward the small bar between the dining room and kitchen, where she helped herself to a glass of white wine. She held up the bottle and waved.

"Actually, I'd rather have a beer."

"Sure thing." She snagged one from the beverage

cooler and twisted the top. Before making her way back, she opened the pantry, looked around, and pulled out a thing of nuts. "I hope you don't mind that I'm grabbing a snack, as well."

"I didn't realize how late it was. I'll order us some dinner. Or, better yet, we can go out if you'd like."

"I'm not in the mood to see people. We can do fast food when you bring me back to the bed and breakfast."

"Nonsense. There is this great little place that does takeout. It's right on the way, and we can eat it on the dock," he said.

"Won't that make Melinda's guests uncomfortable having a cop around all the time?"

He chuckled. "It was only when Emmerson showed up in uniform when I was there, as well as Rhett. Besides, I think half the guests saw us kissing."

"Wonderful. Now, we're simply giving them something to talk about." She set down the beer she'd gotten him from the beverage cooler, along with a tin of nuts. She opted to stand while she sipped her wine and tried not to think about Emmett outside of him doing his cop thing because she'd already undressed him at least five times this evening.

"I was teasing you." He tipped his beer and smiled. "At least about everyone seeing us kiss. That was just Melinda."

"You and she have an interesting relationship."

"That, we do." Emmett nodded.

"You still care about her."

"Of course, I do. But I'm not in love with her anymore if that is where this conversation is going." He arched a brow. "I don't carry a torch for my ex. That ship sailed a long time ago."

"I can tell." Trinity didn't know why she was so desperate to ask him about his fertility. Maybe it was because she felt comfortable talking about the emptiness she felt at losing her child and the ability to have more for the first time in a long while. Sharing that with Melinda earlier had opened Trinity's heart, and spending time with Emmett only filled that space with the anticipation of what it might be like to allow a man inside again. "It's refreshing to see two people who went through a bad breakup get along like you and Melinda do."

"Seems you and Melinda have been getting to know each other." He pushed his chair back and crossed his legs. "Perhaps more than I anticipated."

"She's nice, and she's been looking out for me."

"I'd say she's been telling you things about me." He brought the longneck to his lips and swigged. "She does that when she believes I'm interested in a woman and that girl is a good fit for me."

"How often has that happened?"

"Not often," he said. "But she thinks I'm letting life pass me by."

"Are you?" The last thing she should be doing is meddling in his personal life or trying to get him to tell her his darkest secrets. It was manipulative and rude.

But it would be worse if she came out and told him that Melinda had spilled the beans and telling him her story didn't make sense. Not yet anyway.

"Life hasn't worked out as I planned." He lifted his beer, holding up a finger. "However, that doesn't mean I'm not happy with the life I'm living. You've met a couple of my brothers. They're amazing. And my nieces and nephews are even better. I want for nothing. I'm in a job where I can't imagine doing anything else, and living in a town I love. My world can't get any better."

"What about a family of your own?"

"I'm getting too old for that," he said. "What about you? Do you want to get married? Have kids?"

She shouldn't have gone down this road. It was

too soon to have this conversation with him. Way too soon. She might never have it with him—or anyone for that matter. "I don't know, to be honest. My career as a nurse is important to me. And it's demanding. It's something that Alex, my ex, never understood. I'm not willing to give it up, either." She took a hearty swig before setting her glass down and fiddling with the nuts on the table.

"That's fair," Emmett said. "Even though my parents are divorced, my dad always supported my mom's career."

"That makes a difference."

"For the record, Zadie isn't Jamison's daughter. At least, not biologically. He adopted her." Emmett set his beer on the table and stood. "I think they will have a third, but not the old-fashioned way. They both like the idea of fostering and adopting an older child."

"Bryn told me. I think that's a beautiful way to make a family."

He stood. "I have to agree." He took her into his arms. "I know I said I'd keep my hands and lips to myself, but you don't make it easy."

"I haven't done anything."

"You're in the room." He tucked her hair behind

her ears and gazed into her eyes. "That's a distraction all by itself."

"I'm immune to flattery." Butterflies filled her belly. Flirting had never been her strong suit. Her dry personality always fell short in that department. Alex used to tell her that his friends never understood when she was being funny or serious. She used to tell *him* that unless she was laughing, that should say everything.

Of course, he'd then accused her of barely cracking a smile.

"I doubt that." Emmett held her gaze for a long moment. He had this intense look about him that not only drove her crazy but also made her want to rip off all her clothes right then and there just to see what he'd do. Only, given the way he intently stared at her, she knew he'd call her bluff.

"This isn't a good idea," she whispered.

"It's not a bad one." He pressed his mouth over hers, slipping his hot tongue between her lips.

Involuntarily, she leaned in to his strong frame. His arms wrapped around her in a protective embrace. His fingers dug into her back, massaging her muscles like a pianist tapping at the keys, playing sweet music for a private engagement just for her enjoyment.

It had been a long time since she'd been with a man that'd made her question why she thought she wanted to spend the rest of her life alone. After Alex, she couldn't bring herself to even look at another man. She'd loved him so completely.

And their baby. That loss had broken her in ways she didn't think she'd ever recover from. However, she *did* bounce back thanks to her mother and Ben—no...her dad. Ben was her father in every sense of the word.

But the loss of being able to bear children had stolen a piece of her that she didn't believe she'd ever get back.

However, in Emmett's arms, anything and everything seemed possible.

He deepened the kiss. His hands roamed her back, sending messages to the rest of her body that she wasn't prepared to deal with. She'd ignored this part of being a woman for so long in fear of feeling too much emotion. Any time she allowed herself a taste of being with a man, it was only on the surface. Pure physical release.

This was so much deeper. He was more than a man who could fulfill a need.

He pushed her back against the wall, spreading

her legs, nestling himself between them, putting pressure where she demanded it the most.

A wave of dizziness washed over her, and she clutched at his shoulders. She became desperate to touch every part of him. She tore at his clothing, tugged at his shirt, yanking it over his head.

Breathless, she tossed hers across the room, her bra following.

He stared at her with adoring eyes. His gaze heated her skin like the hot summer sun.

"You're a beautiful woman," he whispered. His lips dotted kisses between her breasts and down her stomach.

She closed her eyes and gave in to her passion. She heaved in a few deep breaths as he rolled her jeans and panties over her hips and down to her ankles. The cool air from the air-conditioning did nothing to bring down her temperature.

He lifted her leg over his shoulder.

"Oh, God," she said with a throaty moan. Threading her fingers through his dark hair, she inhaled sharply. The intake burned her lungs.

Most men she'd been with needed a little guidance, but not Emmett. He understood her body, her mind, and how they worked together. He also made everything about her, not him. That wasn't something she was used to when it came to the lovers she'd picked in the past.

Which had been by design.

The men she chose to spend any time with in bed were the types of guys more impressed by themselves and their performance than their partners. It wasn't that they didn't care if she was satisfied. It was more about how she delivered their desire, not how the two of them came together.

A sudden tightness filled her muscles. Her toes curled, and that sensation crawled up her legs. A tingle and twitch filled her belly. Goosebumps trickled across her skin.

"Emmett," she whispered. Her body jerked and quivered uncontrollably as her climax tore through her body. As soon as she thought it was about to end, a second one hit her just as hard. She tugged at his hair, practically begging him to stop.

He stood, smiling like a big, goofy kid.

She managed to laugh through her heavy pants. "You're quite proud of yourself." Her chest heaved up and down as she tried to take in a deep breath.

He licked his lips before pressing them over her mouth in a slow, passionate kiss.

She groaned.

"I am," he whispered. "But I'm not done yet."

"Neither am I." She desperately needed a break. Not from the encounter but from him keeping all the attention on her body. It was time to flip it. She reached between them, fumbling with his zipper. She managed to undo his pants with relative ease and slipped her hand inside.

"What do you think you're doing?"

He tilted his head and cocked a brow.

"What does it feel like I'm doing?" She curled her fingers around him, squeezing gently but firmly.

His eyes grew wide. "Before this goes any further, we need to have an awkward chat."

"That's so not romantic while I've got this in my hand."

"Maybe this will help." He cupped her breast and took her nipple between his thumb and forefinger.

She gasped. That certainly wasn't helping, but it didn't hurt. "What do we need to discuss?" she managed to ask between raspy breaths.

"In a roundabout way, birth control."

"Why? That's a non-issue for—"

"Melinda told you." It was a statement, not a question. He narrowed his eyes and took a step back, breaking off all physical contact.

"If you had let me finish my sentence, you'd know this isn't about you. It's about me," she said.

"I'm not sure how that can be possible."

"Are you serious?"

"Are you denying that Melinda told you?"

"Not the point," she said.

He zipped his pants and turned his back. "I'll give you a few minutes to get dressed and freshen up before I take you home."

"Are you fucking kidding me?"

"No," he said without glancing over his shoulder. "Perhaps I shouldn't be mad at you. But right now, I'm just pissed off, and I need some space." He snagged his half-drunk beer off the table and padded off into the other room, leaving her standing there, wondering what the fuck had just happened.

Emmett sat out in his backyard, barefoot and shirtless with a fresh beer in one hand and his cell in the other. He stared at it for a long moment. "Fuck it," he mumbled as he set the beer down.

Emmett: *Why the fuck would you tell her that I can't get anyone pregnant?*

He hit send, rested his phone on his leg, and went to take another big swig of his beer. His phone rang. He blew out a puff of air and tapped the answer button, putting it on speaker, knowing that he'd left the screen door open and the kitchen window, as well. If Trinity wanted to listen to this conversation, fine. It would be killing two birds with one stone.

His heart tightened.

"That's not exactly what happened," Melinda said, not bothering with pleasantries. "How did that even come up?"

"None of your business."

"Shit," Melinda said. "You've never been very good at broaching that subject, and I'm not even sure why you do anymore."

"Do I really need to explain it all to you? Sometimes, it's not about birth control. There are other reasons to use those stupid things." Not to mention one particular woman who'd tried to trap him, but Melinda didn't know about her. Very few people did.

"So, you say that and not—oh, hell. I hope you were a lot more sensitive with her feelings than you're being right now because what she went through is a hell of a lot worse than what happened to us."

"What are you talking about?" He lifted his beverage to his lips and chugged. It soured in his belly.

He'd thought he'd come to terms with not being able to father a child. And, really, he had. Only Melinda constantly reminded him that every time he brought up using a condom during sex, he referenced it as birth control instead of protection against sexually transmitted diseases. Just because he regularly got tested—and was clean—didn't mean everyone did.

"Oh, my God. Please tell me you didn't get pissed off and walk away without letting her talk."

"She said enough when she informed me that you broke my trust. And you still haven't answered my question. Why did you tell her? That's my business to share with someone. Not yours. How did it even come up?" He pinched the bridge of his nose. A dull throb started at the base of his neck and crawled up the back of his head to his temples.

"I think you should ask her," Melinda said.

"So do I," Trinity said as she stepped through the sliding glass door, holding a bottle of wine. No glass. Just the open bottle.

He jumped in his seat, spilling his beer. "Shit," he mumbled.

"Especially since I'm right here." Trinity raised the bottle and took a drink.

"Emmett. You'd better listen to what she has to

say. I'm hanging up now," Melinda said, and the phone went dead.

Emmett sucked in a deep breath. He'd thought he had a handle on all this fertility shit, but he didn't, and that pissed him off.

"I never thought I'd call you an asshole, but what you did back there was cruel."

Emmett couldn't argue that point. "You're right. And I'm sorry."

"That doesn't change how much you hurt me. And if I didn't have a tiny understanding of what you might be feeling, I would have called myself a rideshare and wouldn't have even bothered to say one fucking word to you ever again."

He turned and caught her gaze. Emotion filled his heart. The last thing he ever wanted to do was put the kind of pain that stared back at him right in this moment in her eyes. He wanted to pull her into his arms and kiss it away.

But he knew he couldn't. What he'd done could be unforgivable. It was also totally self-sabotage. He cared for her more than he had any other woman he'd dated since Melinda. It didn't matter that they'd just met. His feelings for Trinity consumed him. He couldn't explain it, and he wasn't even going to try.

But he knew how his subconscious operated

because, deep down, his biggest fear since finding out that he couldn't father children was complete and total rejection.

Just like he'd felt from Melinda.

They might have been able to come to an understanding where they could be friends, but that didn't change how he'd felt as if he were less of a man all of a sudden.

Less than human.

"How is it that you understand? And before you answer that, how did you and my ex even get on this conversation?"

"The answer to that is the same." Trinity lifted the bottle and took another swig. Some red wine trickled down her chin. She wiped it with the back of her hand.

He reached for the alcohol, but she jerked her arm back.

"Melinda and I were chatting about a lot of things when we ended up talking about her and Chad doing IVF."

"So, naturally, she told you I was totally against that when we found out I couldn't give her a child."

"For a man who is usually very intuitive, you're being a butthead." She downed more of her beverage. "Our conversation wasn't about you, though she did tell me that was one of the reasons the two of you ended your relationship. But that was only on the tail-end of me telling her that I no longer had the required plumbing to have children." Trinity wiggled the bottle out in front of her.

He tried to take it, but she once again yanked it back close to her body, though only after she drank some more.

"I can't have kids either," she said. "But the worst part is that I know what it's like to have one." She held the bottle up, opened her mouth, and finished it. "And minutes later be told, '*Sorry, it didn't make it, and now we're going to perform an emergency hysterectomy.*'"

"Jesus," Emmett muttered. "I'm surprised you didn't slap me." *Asshole* wasn't a strong enough word to describe his selfish act. Talk about being self-centered.

"That still might happen." She hiccupped.

"Did you just drink that entire bottle?" He reached across her body and snagged it, realizing it wasn't the one he'd opened. Shit.

"Are you drunk-judging me now, too?"

"Not at all," he said as he set the bottle down. How quickly the alcohol hit her system would dictate how much time he had to make a decent apology. Because, pretty soon, she wouldn't remember shit about tonight. He turned her chair and placed his hands on her legs. "I'm sorry about making this all about me and not thinking about your feelings. I got emotional about something that is still obviously an issue for me, and I became blinded by my inadequacies."

She palmed his cheek. "I know those feelings."

"I wish I hadn't reacted the way I did. I can't go back in time and change it. I can only ask for forgiveness."

She covered her mouth and belched.

Not a good sign for what might be in her future for the evening.

"I can forgive you."

"I'm glad," he said. "Now, why don't you let me help you up to bed and get you a big glass of water?" *And a bucket*, but he opted not to mention the latter.

"It's probably best if I not sleep in your bed with you."

"I'll stay in the guest room," he said. "Trust me when I say you'll be more comfortable in my room. Where the bathroom is closer."

She belched again. "Okay." She pushed herself to a standing position, only she wobbled on her legs and fell forward into his arms. "Oops," she said.

He scooped her up and carried her into the house and down the hallway to the master bedroom.

His house wasn't on the water, but he lived in town, and he enjoyed the easy access to restaurants and the beach. Not to mention, he owned it outright. If he ever *did* get married, which wasn't likely at this stage in his life, he would absolutely give it up and buy a place on the water or a bigger house outside of town. But for now, it worked for him.

"Here you go." Carefully, he tugged off her jeans and tucked her under the sheets. He sat on the edge of the bed and brushed her hair away from her face. He'd fucked up big this time. "I'm really sorry. My behavior was horrible. When you said birth control was a non-issue, I shouldn't have assumed it was about me."

"I would have done the same thing if the tables were turned," she said softly.

"I know you might not remember this part of the evening in the morning, and I'll likely have to repeat it, but I'm sorry you lost your baby. That breaks my heart."

"Thank you." She took his hand and pressed it against the center of her chest. "I'm sorry we didn't get to finish."

He chuckled. "We have plenty of time for that."

He leaned over and kissed her forehead. "Close your eyes and sleep."

Her lashes fluttered. "The room is spinning." She bolted upright, flipping the covers to the side and then stumbling toward the bathroom.

It would be a long night.

11

Trinity groaned. She couldn't bring herself to even blink, much less move. Her entire body ached, and her head throbbed with the worst hangover she'd ever had.

She swallowed and nearly gagged at the wretched taste in her mouth. It was as if she'd eaten food right from a dumpster that had been sitting in the sun for five days and doused with antifreeze.

"Ugh." She rolled from her stomach to her side and hit something solid with her back.

"Well, hello," a familiar voice said.

Carefully, as not to upset the precarious balance in her head, she glanced over her shoulder.

Emmett lay propped up on a bunch of pillows

with a book in one hand and a mug of coffee in the other.

Her stomach churned. She wasn't sure it was a good one, or one that would send her running for the bathroom.

Again.

"How long have you been there?"

"All night," he said. "Someone had to hold your hair back."

"Oh, God." She covered her face and buried it in the mattress. "I remember drinking wine right from the bottle. I remember we sorted things out, a little bit. But it gets sketchy real quick."

"You were angry with me, though I can't say as I blame you."

The bed shifted.

She placed her hands palm down and made sure her stomach could handle the movement before she sat up.

So far, so good.

She found the hair tie that she always had around her wrist and managed to pull her hair up into a messy bun on top of her head. It almost helped with the headache.

Almost.

"I was hurt and a little humiliated," she said.

"I can understand." He set his book on the nightstand and handed her his coffee.

She palmed it and sipped. "Oh. That's good." Her stomach accepted it, and that was a bit of a surprise. Her eyes adjusted to the bright lights. She glanced around the room, finding his cell propped up on a charging station. "It's eleven?"

"You needed to sleep," he said. "You were vomiting until five."

"Why are you still in bed?" She glanced down and realized he wasn't under the covers, and he was fully dressed.

"I've been in and out, checking on you."

"If I weren't still upset with you, I'd say that was sweet." She palmed the mug and lifted it to her nose. The scent calmed her stomach. "Why did you automatically assume my saying we didn't need birth control had to do with you? For all you knew, I could have been on the pill. Besides, you didn't even let me finish my sentence. You totally interrupted me."

"You're right on all accounts. I have no excuse, and I'm not going to make any. What I did was wrong. However, I would like a chance to explain how I was feeling and what went through my mind and why, because it's not only because I was told I can never father a child."

"I believe that's fair." She set the coffee on the nightstand and twisted her body so she could focus her attention on Emmett.

"Having a family—children—used to be really important to me," he said. "When Melinda and I got engaged, we didn't want to wait. We started trying right away. We used to joke she would be waddling down the aisle, and we didn't care. But month after month, it didn't happen, and we kept not setting a date as we started to go through the process of finding out why. We discovered quickly that it was me. I saw a specialist who crushed our dreams. But he mentioned a sperm donor, and Melinda was all over that. I was grappling with my emotions and couldn't believe she wanted to start looking right away."

"I can understand you wanting to take a beat."

"I wanted nothing to do with the idea of raising another man's child."

"That's not how that works," Trinity said. "It's no different than adopting."

"I tend to have a bit of a jealous streak. But, yes, I get that now. However, it took me a while to process, and Melinda no time to move on to the next step in having a child. But that's not the issue I had last night. I had no idea what you'd gone through. I'd been left in the dark." He took her hand and kissed her palm. "The first girl I dated after Melinda and I broke up wasn't from around here. That was by design. It was a rebound, and I told Bridget—that was her name—that I wasn't looking for anything serious. Unfortunately, she was. After about four months, she came to me and told me she was pregnant and that it was mine."

"I take it she didn't know about your situation?"

Emmett shook his head. "Because I had issues with my manhood, I used those damn condoms less because of sexual disease, though that's always a good idea. Still, I did it more because it made me feel like it was still possible, even though it wasn't."

"I can understand that." She glanced down at her stomach as she placed a hand over it. "For months after I had my hysterectomy, I constantly checked for my period. I thought every little pain in my belly was cramps." She laughed, though it wasn't a funny, ha-ha, laugh; more of a pathetic, sarcastic one. "I wouldn't have sex because I was worried that I couldn't have an orgasm without a uterus."

"We know that's not true."

Her cheeks heated.

"What did you say to the woman you were seeing?" Trinity needed to bring things back to the topic at hand.

"She rendered me speechless for about ten minutes, which is nearly impossible to do," Emmett said. "I stood at my front door and stared at her, not saying a single word while she explained what she expected."

"Dare I ask?"

"Oh. It was good because she expected everything, including the diamond ring. She even had suitcases in her car, expecting to move right in with me. So, imagine her surprise when I told her that it was one hundred percent impossible for me to knock her up. I slammed the door in her face. The next day, she threatened me, and I offered up my medical records. That shut her up real quick."

"I have to ask. Was she really pregnant?"

"She was," Emmett said. "Last I heard, she's with the father, but I honestly don't keep track. Jamison is always telling me that I keep the condom discussion the way I do because I have trust issues and that it's almost a test for the women I date."

"I like Jamison." Trinity stared at their intertwined fingers. "And I think he's right, but I would too if those things had happened to me."

"Thank you for that." He leaned closer and tilted her head with his free hand. "But that still doesn't excuse the way I treated you. I'm ashamed of my behavior, and I'd like to make it up to you."

"If you're looking to take up where we left off, that's going to have to wait," she said. "I feel like shit."

"We might want to slow that down a bit." He kissed her cheek. "I was thinking more like a romantic boat ride at sunset. What do you say?"

"Only if I can use that big tub of yours to soak in before I head back to the bed and breakfast."

"You can stay right here until about six." He brushed his lips gently over her mouth in a tender, sweet kiss. "I need to go into the station. My mom has some things she wants to go over with me regarding your father's case."

"Should I come?"

"No." He kissed her nose. "You rest. If you feel the need to do something, there's still all that paperwork on my dining room table, and I'll leave my tablet for you. The code to get into it is eight-six-seven-five."

"Three-oh-nine," she said with a giggle.

"You know the song," he said. "I'm impressed."

"That's really where you got the code?"

He nodded.

"Why?"

"I'm not telling."

"There's got to be a Jenny in your life somewhere," she said. "Oh, my God. You lost your virginity to a girl named Jenny."

"Nope." He shook his head. "But that song was playing, and that's all I'm going to say about that." He kissed her. Hard. Passionately.

Rendering her speechless.

"I'll see you later. Have a nice afternoon." He jumped from the bed and raced out of the room.

"Wow," she whispered. That certainly got rid of her hangover in a heartbeat. She leaned back and closed her eyes, allowing all the sensations to soak into her skin. She didn't want to miss a single one. Unfortunately, the sound of a cell vibrating on the nightstand cut it short.

She sat up and stared at her phone charging next to her—it was sweet of him to do that. Kathy's contact information flashed on the screen, and she was the last person Trinity wanted to deal with right now.

However, Kathy would be relentless if she didn't take the call. And, truth be told, she was only being a good friend.

A little overbearing and smothering, but she meant well.

Trinity blew out a puff of air and picked up the phone. "Hey, Kath."

"Oh, my God, girl. Where the hell have you been? I've been worried sick about you."

Trinity didn't have a lot of close girlfriends. It took her a while to make friends, but Kathy had wormed her way into her life. More because Kathy was aggressive, but she was also nice and meant well. However, this was over the top. "I've been busy, Kath. I can't call and text you the second you reach out to me."

"Don't be like that. You told me once that you can get obsessed with things to the point where it becomes unhealthy. You told me that you let things get out of hand when you tried to find your father, and that it was for nothing because you did nothing with the information."

Trinity groaned. Kathy was right. Not only had she said that, but it was also true. She'd spent months trying to track him down. Not only that, she'd used up half her savings. And for what?

At the end of the day, she'd never contacted her biological father.

"This is different." Trinity swung her legs to the side of the bed. Her stomach sloshed in angry protest. She paused, giving her body a chance to recover. "I'm not the only one who believes there could be an issue with the way all this was handled."

"Are you sure you're not becoming a bit preoccupied with him, as well? You do tend to attach yourself to men quickly."

"Did you seriously just say that to me?" She pushed herself to a standing position. Her legs wobbled slightly as her head pounded. She breathed slowly. "Since when have you known me to even be involved with a man? I barely date."

"You told me how quickly you got involved with Alex and how hard it was for you to let him go. Your mother agrees."

"You spoke to my mother?" Trinity eased to the edge of the bed and placed a hand over her upset stomach. "Why would you do that? If anyone has issues with being all-consumed by something right now, it's you. I have to be honest. I don't appreciate you calling my mom. I don't need her freaking out, and I find what you did a little *Single White Female*."

"Now I'm hurt and insulted," Kathy said with an indignant tone. "Has anything changed? Can anyone prove that Jeff Allen didn't murder those men?"

"Not yet," Trinity said. "But Emmett's working on it.

"Then why don't you let him deal with it and come home?"

Trinity was tired of having the same conversation with Kathy. "If it's going to be about this every time we chat, I'm not going to pick up the phone. I'm going to see this through until I'm satisfied that my father was at least given a fair shot, even in death."

"You're only going to end up getting hurt."

"I'm prepared for the worst," Trinity said. "But this is something I have to do. I'm sorry. I've got to go. I'll let you know if I find out anything."

"All right. Be good to yourself, okay?"

"I will." Trinity ended the call and chucked her phone across the bed. She liked Kathy, she really did, but it was time to set some better boundaries. At least, for the time being.

However, right now, she needed to find some hangover food and look at some of the files that Emmett had left.

That song by Tommy TuTone played in her mind. Wonderful. There was no way she was getting that out of her head now.

Nor would she stop thinking about being with Emmett.

It was going to be a long afternoon.

Emmett didn't like lying to Trinity. Not one bit. But she was in no shape to sit in a car and possibly deal with a confrontation with an eyewitness. Besides, he was crossing a line as a police officer, and he didn't need to drag a civilian into it, even if he were doing it for Trinity.

"Are you sure you want to do this?" Rhett asked. "You can leave the dirty work to me if you want."

"No. I need to see this one through." He parked his SUV in front of a townhouse in Coral Springs, a community north of Fort Lauderdale.

"Is this because you were the last one to see Jeff alive, or because you have feelings for Trinity?"

"Both," he admitted. He had no reason to lie to Rhett—or anyone in his family. He might not get down and dirty with all the details, but he could use a friend right about now, and while Rhett was a ladies' man, he'd had his heart crushed once in the past. He understood better than most why Emmett had been so guarded the last few years. "I don't know what the fuck is wrong with me. Everything is happening too fast with her, and I can't keep my head above water."

"That's how it was with Melinda," Rhett said.

"But every time I've asked one specific question, you can't answer it or say you don't know. I think you need to re-examine that one."

Emmett didn't need his brother to say more. He knew exactly what he was talking about.

Had Melinda really been THE ONE? At first, Emmett had been adamant that, yes, she'd been his one and only. But everyone, including the therapist he'd seen for a brief time, constantly asked him why they'd never set a date.

Ever.

They had been engaged for four years and had never gone through the motions of setting a date. There was always an excuse. First, it was stuff going on with her family and the bed and breakfast. Then it was stuff with him and them trying to have a baby. Each month, they waited to see if they were pregnant because if it happened, they would have had to decide if they really wanted her to be expecting during the ceremony or if they should wait.

Of course, each month the bad news came, and that halted the wedding plans while the process started all over again.

As Emmett examined their relationship, he began to see the same pattern that everyone else did, and that was that perhaps Melinda and he weren't as madly in love with each other as they thought. Maybe they weren't perfect for each other. Because when he saw Chad and Melinda together, it warmed his heart.

Emmett blew out a puff of air. "It's hard to admit that Melinda and I weren't right for each other after spending six years together, but I've settled into that realization."

Rhett gave him a brotherly shoulder squeeze. "We all know you loved her, but it wouldn't have lasted forever."

"I can see that now. We both can."

"Trinity's more your type. She's a little less high-strung, and I like how she handles things. She's down to earth. Honest. And she doesn't take shit from anyone. I think she's perfect for you."

"Do you have any idea how nuts that sounds?"

"No odder than how much you thought that chick Shelby was perfect for me, when not only did I barely know her, but she was simply a one-night stand."

Emmett tossed his head back and burst out laughing. "You spent three weeks with her holed up in some cheap hotel room in Key West."

"It wasn't cheap." Rhett waggled his finger under

Emmett's nose. "And just because it was more than an evening doesn't mean it was meant to be a lifetime of love."

"Regardless, she was hot."

"Yeah, she was," Rhett said. "I kind of wish I knew where she lived. I wouldn't mind seeing her again."

"You never got her number?"

"Oh. I did. But I never called her. I was still upset over Krista, and then like a fucking fool, I deleted her contact." He shrugged. "If it were meant to be, we would have crossed paths again."

Emmett had never heard those words from his brother before. Ten years ago, it had only been about Krista. He rarely brought up Shelby, and whenever anyone else did, he chuckled and treated it like she was another notch in his belt like any of the other women he'd dated in the last five years.

But now, Emmett wondered if maybe they'd gotten it wrong and it wasn't Krista who had his brother's heart all tied up in knots.

Maybe it was Shelby.

"Besides, we're not talking about me. This is about you and Trinity," Rhett said. "I can't imagine what it must have been like to find out at sixteen that her father murdered her mother's lover. That's harsh. Why is she so sure he didn't kill these men?"

"The same reasons we are," Emmett admitted. "It doesn't add up. Plain and simple."

"She's right. Nothing makes sense." Rhett leaned forward and pulled out a folder. "This guy, Tony, told the police that he saw someone who matches the description of Jeff's sketch at the scene where one of the victims was found. He also said he saw the same man talking with a different victim at the bar he works at. What's interesting to me is that the second victim was murdered two days after Jeff left the area, at least according to Jeff's timeline."

"I wish he'd left detailed notes." Emmett hit the ignition button, shutting off the engine. "Are you ready?"

"Sure am."

Emmett slipped from behind the steering wheel. It felt strange to be going to question someone when not in uniform. It didn't matter that he was carrying his service weapon and his badge. It still felt different.

"Who's taking the lead?" Rhett asked.

"You can. For now."

Emmett was also used to working with his mom, Nathan, or Emmerson—all control freaks.

One his boss.

The other two older.

Well, Rhett was older, too. But he wasn't a cop. It was a different dynamic—most days.

Rhett chuckled. "You mean I get to knock on the door and ask if Tony is available?"

"Something like that."

Emmett glanced over his shoulder, checking out the neighborhood. It was a nice one—mid-range houses and condos. Decent cars lined the streets. And it was only five miles from the beach.

Rhett rang the bell.

It took about two minutes before an older gentleman with long, white hair and a matching beard answered the door.

"Can I help you?" the man asked.

"Are you Tony?" Rhett asked.

"That depends on who wants to know." Tony held the door open.

"My name's Rhett. This is my brother, Emmett. I left you a message this morning about your statement regarding two murders."

"Oh. Yeah. I didn't call you back," Tony said. "Pretty ballsy of you to just show up without an invite."

"I'm not sure if you've seen the news or not. A man was shot in Lighthouse Cove," Emmett said. "He was wanted in connection with the same murders you came forward and said you had some information regarding."

"I saw it," Tony said.

"We're not sure he's the guy," Rhett said. "We want to know what you think."

"That fed told me I was mistaken. That my account was wrong," Tony said with disdain dripping from every syllable. "She told me my statement was useless."

"We disagree." Rhett held pulled a copy of the sketch from his pocket and unfolded it. "Is this the man you saw?"

"Yeah. That's him. Swear to God. He took meetings in my bar. I didn't keep track of them all because I didn't know what they were about at first. And I doubt they were all hired for the same thing. But I can tell you about one of them. Because it was a woman I know. She wanted to hire him to kill her husband."

Emmett stole a glance at his brother. That wasn't in the report they'd gotten.

"You told the agent who took your statement that?" Rhett asked.

"No," Tony said. "I couldn't toss that poor girl under the bus. Her asshole of a husband beat the shit out of her on a regular basis. Bastard would have deserved it if it ever happened. But it didn't. She didn't have enough money." Tony ran his hand over his long beard. "The jerk hitman would have done it for sexual favors."

"Where's this young woman now?"

Tony smiled. "She's a waitress in my bar. Her now soon-to-be ex-husband is in prison."

"I take it you had something to do with that?" Emmett asked.

"Damn fucking right," Tony said. "But I worry about when that man gets out. He's only in for three years. He's a real piece of work, and if she doesn't get rid of him for good, she'll be the one in the morgue."

"We can help you with that," Emmett said. "I'm a cop, and my brother here is a private investigator. Once her divorce is final, the best thing she can do is relocate."

"I know. But that's easier said than done," Tony said.

"We know people who've been able to do it successfully." Emmett shifted his weight. He was tired of standing on the front step of this townhouse. "We'd be happy to help you through the process and put you in touch with those who can help her financially, too."

"You'd do that? Why? What's in it for you?"

Emmett tried not to laugh. "I told you. I'm a police officer. It's my job to protect and serve."

Tony shook his head. "First, that goes above and beyond the call of duty. And, second, most cops are shady. Sorry. That's just that truth. I learned that after trying to do the right thing and then having some bitch come in, call me a liar, and look me up and down like I'm some criminal based on the way I look."

"We believe you," Emmett said. "And we'd like to hear what you have to say about it."

"What difference does it make? I read that Robash woman officially closed the case." Tony folded his arms across his chest.

"She may have, but we're working on reopening it. We don't believe that Jeff Allen killed those men. Our working theory is that someone set him up." Rhett held up the sketch. "This man. We just don't understand why. Or how Robash is tied to it. We were hoping you could help."

"Can we come in?" Emmett asked.

"Sure." Tony stepped aside, pulling the door open wider. "I have a half hour before I need to leave for work."

"We appreciate the time." Emmett was a tad surprised by Tony's taste in décor. For someone who looked like a biker, his house had a very different feel with its coral and teal colors. His cloth sofa was white with an octopus throw pillow on one side and a sea turtle on the other. It reminded Emmett of a little seaside store down in Boca that his mother liked to shop in but that her future husband hated.

"I never understood why the FBI agent decided that what I saw wasn't helpful. That man—the one in the sketch—he hung out in my bar a lot."

"When was the last time you saw him?" Rhett asked. "And what was his name? Do you know?"

"He went by Bugsy. When pressed for a real name or a last name, he never gave one. He hasn't been in my bar in months. And, believe me, I looked for him. He tended to make my patrons uncomfortable." Tony waved his hand in front of a couple of recliners and a sofa in the family room that opened to the kitchen. "Can I get you gentlemen a drink?"

"No. But thank you," Emmett said, and Rhett shook his head. "What was it about him that bothered people?"

"His attitude and the way he talked about the shit he did in the military. I served, and we don't talk about that shit the way he did." Tony leaned on a stool by the kitchen.

Emmett opted for a seat on the sofa while his brother stood near the coffee table, checking the place out.

"At first, I thought he was a wannabe bullshitter trying to pick up women, but the more he came in, the more I realized he was using my place of business to meet people who wanted to hire him." Tony scratched the side of his face. "I thought the police were onto him because I saw a couple of undercover cops come in and talk to him, but weeks went by, and nothing happened."

"How is it that you ended up seeing him near one of the crime scenes?" Rhett asked.

"I followed him," Tony said matter-of-factly. "It looked like he was casing out the area. Less than two days later, a man was dead. Bugsy was in my bar and laughed when the news came on, discussing the case. He actually thought it was funny. I went to the cops with what I knew and thought they had taken me seriously, but I kept seeing Bugsy coming around. Then a second man was murdered, and that's when the feds came into the picture. Of course, it was all linked to this Adultery Killer case. The only thing I could think was that maybe Bugsy had an alibi for the murders down in Miami or something. But still, it just all seemed too odd to me. And then to be dismissed..." Tony shrugged. "Maybe Bugsy didn't kill that man, but he isn't a good person, either."

"Do you happen to have any pictures of him? Anything we can use to try to find out who he is?"

"I did, but my bar was vandalized two weeks after that fed told me my intel wasn't good enough. Someone broke into my safe and took the images I had of him, along with about twenty grand, some of my wife's jewelry, and a few other random things." Tony waved his finger. "I told the police I didn't think the break-in was a coincidence, but nothing was ever done, and they never found out who did it."

"You believe it was this Bugsy guy?" Emmett asked.

"Or someone connected to him," Tony said. "However, I do have something that might interest you." Tony pushed from his stool. "I thought the feds might want to match his handwriting to a note he left for my friend who thought about hiring him. But they believed that man who got shot the other day was their guy, so they basically blew me off."

"We'd love to take a look at it," Rhett said.

"I can give you a copy." Tony hurried across the room. "I'll also give you my card with my friend's contact information on the back. She could really use some help and guidance. I'd hate for her to fall back into the same trap when that asshole husband of hers gets out."

"We're happy to help." Emmett pulled out one of his cards from his back pocket. "This has my personal cell. Call anytime."

"Thanks. I appreciate it." Tony handed Emmett a copy of the note, along with his friend's contact information.

Immediately, Emmett noticed some similarities between the note and the ones that had been left on the victims. But he was no handwriting expert. "We'll be in touch." His heart jumped to the back of his throat. He couldn't call this a break in the case, but it was enough that he knew they were on the right track.

He stepped outside. The humid air clung to his pores as he jogged around the hood of his vehicle.

"What do you make of a hired gun being our killer?" Rhett asked the second he pulled the seatbelt across his lap.

"It means we're most likely not dealing with a serial killer. Which means we need to look at this case from a different perspective." Emmett glanced over his shoulder before pulling out onto the street. "The victims without the notes were most likely killed by someone else and not related. We need to go back and figure out who would want to frame Jeff and why?"

"What about his ex-wife? He killed her lover."

"She's happily married to the man who adopted Trinity." Emmett's mind went into overdrive. He churned everything over in his mind, playing out different scenarios, but nothing made sense. Too many pieces of the puzzle were missing.

"Okay, so not Sandy or Ben," Rhett said. "What about Paul's family?"

"He had a wife and two children. A boy who was five, and a girl who was two at the time." Emmett racked his brain for their names. "I believe it was Shawn and Rayna—shit. That makes so much fucking sense. They're pissed off that they lost their father. One of them sees or finds Jeff and sets him up by using the premise that Jeff is re-killing their father in his mind. It's genius."

Rhett pulled out his tablet and tapped on the screen. "Nothing on Rayna. As a matter of fact, it's like she doesn't exist."

"How is that possible? Even I have an internet footprint, and I don't have a single social media account."

"That's because you're listed as a police officer on the county website," Rhett said. "Same with Mom,

Nathan, and Emmerson. But some people are a little more difficult to find. However, give me a day or two, and I will."

"Okay. What about Shawn?"

"He's an entirely different story. Shawn is all over social media. He's rich as fuck. Has private jets, boats, houses all over the place. His Insta feed reads like a who's who of Wall Street."

"What does he do?"

"Venture capitalist," Rhett said. "He also has some foundation that helps out young entrepreneurs. His website talks about him being orphaned at a young age when his father was murdered and later when his mother died from a drug overdose."

"That's tough."

"They were both raised by their maternal grandmother. They didn't have a lot of money. However, Shawn scored ridiculously high on every aptitude test known to man and got himself a scholarship, where he ended up graduating in three years before getting a master's degree. From there, he became one of the richest young men in the country. At first glance, he's the poster child for hard work."

"What's the ugly underbelly?" Emmett asked.

"Some articles connecting him to criminal

activity. He's been investigated for securities fraud, though nothing came of it. And there is some question as to how he came into all his money. But it looks more like people are trying to find faults where there might not be any."

"Still, it sounds like we might have a suspect as to who would hire a hitman to frame Jeff."

"Not to mention having the resources to do it," Rhett said. "But that means buying off Robash. While she's a piece of work and will do what she needs to get ahead, I struggle with seeing her go that far."

"I know what you mean." Emmett eased onto the interstate. "She's aggressive, but from the interactions I've had with her, I get the impression she's more willing to bend the rules to get ahead, not blatantly break them."

"Perhaps, but desperate people do some strange things when their backs are against the wall. And she could have another reason," Rhett said. "Why don't you let me take a crack at her?"

"No. I think we should release Mom on her."

"Oh. That's just mean."

Emmett laughed. "How do you feel about taking a trip to Manhattan to check out Shawn."

"I'd be happy to," Rhett said. "What about Bugsy?"

"Phil Conway spent some time in the military, and Lucy Ann's father works for the Department of Defense. I'm going to pull them into the loop."

"Sounds like a plan."

Emmett glanced at the digital clock on the dashboard. He punched the gas. He had thirty minutes to make it back to Lighthouse Cove for his date with Trinity. He'd fill her in on what they'd learned, and, hopefully, after the business portion of the evening ended, he'd be able to show her that he wasn't a total asshole and make up for his bad behavior from last night.

12

Trinity tossed a sweatshirt into a bag just in case it got chilly out on the water. She glanced at her watch. Emmett had mentioned that he would be late. Something about meeting with his mom and his other brother, Nathan, about the case. She couldn't be mad at him about that, and if they didn't go out for a boat ride, it wouldn't be the end of the world.

She should put the brakes on anything happening between them anyway. No matter how attracted she was to Emmett or how much she liked him, the last thing she needed was to start another long-distance relationship with a man she barely knew.

Wondering how much longer Emmett would be, she patted down her pockets, looking for her cell.

Shit. She'd left it in her purse in the main room of the bed and breakfast. She still couldn't get over how beautiful this place was, or how easily Melinda managed it. From all appearances, it looked as if she did it all by herself. Her staff was almost invisible.

Trinity tossed her bag over her shoulder and headed down the massive staircase. Her headache had finally disappeared, but only after eating the biggest, greasiest cheeseburger topped with a fried egg and some onion rings.

Best hangover food ever.

Along with a couple of diet sodas loaded with caffeine and at least a gallon of water.

"There you are." Melinda stood at the bottom of the stairs with two people—a man and a woman. "I want you to meet Phil and Lucy Ann Conway. They own the diner where your dad was shot."

Trinity paused. Her heart tightened. When she saw the footage on the news, the only people she'd focused on were her dad, Emmett, his mom, and Agent Robash. She'd never really thought about everyone else in the restaurant that day.

"Emmett sent us over to talk with you." Phil held a small briefcase in his hand. "He mentioned that he was on his way but might be late."

"I haven't checked my phone in the last hour,"

Trinity admitted. "So, if he tried to call or text me about all this, I haven't seen it."

"That's okay," Phil said. "Melinda, can we use your office?"

"Sure. You know the way. Can I bring you a snack and some drinks?"

Trinity held up her hands. "I don't need anything."

"We're good, too," Phil said.

Trinity set her bag by the bottom of the stairs and followed the couple down a long hallway and into a part of the house she'd never seen. It was like the back side of Disney. The part the patrons didn't get to see and Disney did its best to cover up.

Phil opened a white door with tinted glass. Inside was a small home office that faced the water on the opposite side of the pool. Phil took a seat behind the desk and set the briefcase on the wood top, taking out a stack of papers before putting the case on the floor next to his feet.

His wife made herself comfortable on one of the chairs in front of the desk, so Trinity took the other.

Lucy Ann reached over and took her hand. "I'm sorry for your loss."

"Thank you."

"I was at the diner when your father was shot. I'm

going to apologize now for making rash judgments about him, but regardless of what anyone thought of him, he didn't deserve that," Lucy Ann said.

Trinity nodded. She wasn't quite sure what to make of Lucy Ann's statement, but she appreciated the honesty.

"Let me give you a little background about me." Phil rested his hands on the desk. "When I was eighteen, I joined the Navy, where I met Lucy Ann's father. He talked me into becoming a SEAL, which was one of the best decisions I ever made—next to marrying Lucy Ann, of course." He shifted his gaze to his wife and smiled.

It had to be one of the sweetest, most sincere things Trinity had ever witnessed.

"I retired after I got my twenty years in so I could spend more time with my family. I still have a lot of contacts in the military. And my father-in-law, Lucy Ann's dad, is high up in the Department of Defense." He tapped his finger on the wood top. "That sketch your father made is of a Navy man."

"How can you tell?" Trinity asked.

"He can't," Lucy Ann said. "But we sent the sketch to my dad, who had a buddy of his run it through a facial recognition program. We got a hit."

Trinity stiffened her spine. "Who?"

"The man's name is Gary Malone, but he goes by Bugsy," Phil said. "He left the Navy about six years ago. He doesn't have a great record. Most of his superior officers had nothing but negative things to say."

"Why was he following my dad?" Trinity asked.

"Our working theory is that someone hired him to make it look like your father was killing those men. When in reality, he was the one doing the murdering." Phil leaned back and swirled the chair left and right. "The question is who. Jack, my father-in-law, did some digging into Bugsy's background."

A tap at the door startled Trinity. She jerked, twisting her back.

"What did I miss?" Emmett asked as he stepped across the threshold, quickly closing the door. He stood behind Trinity, placing his hands on her shoulders and massaging.

"Not much," Phil said. "But I'm glad you're here. The information Jack obtained about Bugsy is interesting, to say the least."

"We know he had some disciplinary issues while enlisted," Emmett said.

"It goes much deeper than that." Phil tapped his fingers on top of the stack of papers in a rhythmic motion. "I'm surprised he lasted as long as he did in the Navy. He wanted to be a SEAL." Phil handed some of the papers to Emmett. "But he did poorly on his Computerized Special Operations and Resiliency Test."

"What's that?" Trinity asked, wanting to understand everything that Phil was talking about.

"It measures personality traits, psychological resilience, and things like that so the Navy can decide if you're mentally prepared for the training and the job. It's put together with performance testing—running and swimming—to see if you have both the mental and physical capacity to be a SEAL. It's only one part of a group of tests," Phil said.

"What did that test say about this Bugsy guy?" Trinity glanced between Phil and Emmett.

"He had no problem with the physical aspect," Emmett said as he thumbed through the stapled grouping of papers. "But it seems he had some issues with his personality and was rejected from the SEAL program because the Navy felt he wasn't a team player."

"That's a nice way of saying that those in charge felt Bugsy was the kind of man whose outside-of-the-box thinking was reckless and not innovative," Phil said. "And that he's difficult to work with. On a

SEAL team, that's not a desirable trait. Hell, it's doesn't fly anywhere in the military."

Trinity's head spun with all the information. She wasn't sure what to make of all of it. Never in a million years would her mind have gone in this direction on its own. She turned to Lucy Ann. "How did your father get all this? And why do we believe this man would frame my dad? I'm not able to wrap my brain around this."

"My dad is high up in the DoD," Lucy Ann said. "When we told him what happened, and Emmett gave him what he found out today, he did some checking."

"What did you find out?" She looked at Emmett.

He sat on the edge of the desk, facing her, and took her hand. "Right now, Rhett is on a plane to Manhattan to have a little chat with Shawn Lewis."

"Paul's son? As in the kid of the man my dad killed when I was a baby?" Her chest tightened. Heat filled her veins like a lit match dropping into a full tank of gas. "You think he's holding a grudge and wanted my father back in prison?"

"Exactly," Emmett said.

"That makes so much sense. I can't believe I didn't think of it," Trinity said. "Wasn't there a daughter, too?"

"We can't find her. Anywhere." Emmett released her hand and stood. "We don't even have a picture of her, except for when she was a young girl. There's nothing about her on the internet. We checked passport and license records and she doesn't have one."

"My father is having his contacts check to see if she possibly changed her name, but that's not easily hidden. It's public record unless it's done illegally," Lucy Ann said.

"It's possible if she wanted to fly under the radar, but she'd have to know people, and it would cost money," Phil said.

"Shawn's wealthy," Emmett stood in front of the big window with his arms folded. "They could be in on it together, so it would be nice to know what she looks like and have a last-known address. The one we have is her grandparents', and they have since passed away."

"Let's hope your brother finds out something in New York." Phil stood and stretched out his arm, taking his wife's hand. "We'd best get going. Our babysitter has a date tonight."

"Thanks for all your help," Emmett said.

Trinity slumped back on the chair and stared at

the ceiling. "Is this all for real? I mean, I feel like I'm stuck in an episode of *The Twilight Zone.*"

Emmett lifted her from the chair and took her into his arms. He held her close to his chest and ran his arms up and down her back.

"There is something else I need to tell you, and it's not going to be easy for you to hear," Emmett said.

She stared into his kind, caring eyes. They conveyed a strength and gentleness that touched her soul. She felt safe in his embrace, and she knew it wasn't a fleeting moment. "What is it?"

"The autopsy on your dad came back. He had terminal cancer."

She let out a gasp and covered her mouth.

"It makes more sense to me now why he walked out of the diner the way he did. Robash still moved too quickly, but I suspect if she hadn't, he might have done something aggressive to make them trigger-happy."

"How do you know he knew about the cancer? He was homeless and couldn't afford healthcare."

"We found a paper trail to a clinic in Miami. My mom was able to get a warrant for the medical records and spoke to the doctor who mentioned that your dad wanted to make his way north one last time to see his little girl."

She dropped her head to Emmett's shoulder and sobbed. The tears burned on her cheeks. The pain ripped through her heart. "I can't believe this."

"I won't ever lie to you," Emmett whispered. "The doctor said your father only had weeks left, and that was six months ago."

She sucked in a deep breath, doing her best to calm herself. "Thank you," she managed.

He put a finger under her chin and tilted her head. "I believe one hundred percent that your father didn't kill anyone, and I'm not going to rest until I prove it."

Emmett carried the tray of comfort food up the stairs. He crossed the threshold of Trinity's room and set everything on the desk before closing the door.

"I'm sorry for ruining your boating plans." Trinity lay on the bed with a glass of wine, her legs stretched out and ankles crossed. Her eyes were a little puffy from crying.

"You haven't ruined anything." He brought the

food over to the bed and set it in the middle before climbing onto the mattress and pouring himself a small glass of red.

"You don't have to stay with me. I promise I'll be okay."

"I'm sure you will be, but I'm not going anywhere." He tapped his glass against hers and winked. "No way would I feel right about leaving you alone after the day you've had." He hated that he'd had to tell her about her dad's cancer. Maybe someone else would have kept that information from her, but she had a right to know.

"I wonder if he was in pain," she whispered. "What did he look like to you?"

"Not well, to be honest. But I made an assumption about him being homeless and how thin he was."

"That's fair," she said. "I tried to find him before he was accused of being the Adultery Killer."

"You mentioned that." Emmett nibbled on the sandwiches that Melinda's staff had made. God, he missed homemade bread.

"My parents thought I was obsessing over what had happened to him. If he was still alive and where he was living. So did my friend, Kathy."

"But you found him."

She nodded. "When it came out that he was the number one suspect in the murders, I thought about trying to find him again."

"Why didn't you?"

She fiddled with one of the sandwich squares, pulling a few pieces off and tossing them back to the plate instead of putting them into her mouth.

If she were going to get nutrients, he would have to feed her himself.

"I spent a lot of money the first time and didn't have the resources to do it again. I also didn't want to upset and worry my parents. The more the bodies piled up, the more the news coverage pointed toward Jeff Allen being the killer." She picked up a second sandwich square and picked it apart. "A reporter did a three-part series on my dad. He talked all about how he'd killed Paul and how he hadn't seemed remorseful at all during the sentencing. He showed pictures and footage." She glanced up. "But I still couldn't wrap my brain around him being guilty. Not of these murders. I know he did a bad thing. I'm not making excuses for him. He killed Paul. He deserved to go to prison. However, he paid his debt. In full. It doesn't make sense to me that he would randomly start killing again."

"I agree." He picked up a bite and placed it into

her mouth. "So, how many times did you try to find your dad?"

"Once. But, sometimes when I decide to do something, I become too focused. I get so lost in the task that I forget about everything else. Except maybe work. My parents worry about me because of my ex, Alex. They thought I nearly lost myself because of him."

Emmett continued to feed Trinity and, thankfully, she didn't protest. She needed the nutrients. "I'm sorry if I'm bringing up painful memories. But was the obsession before or after your loss and breakup?"

"It was after," she said. "The fact that Alex could move on so quickly and act as if what we'd gone through barely mattered, well…I didn't understand it. I was still grieving the loss of our child and any future kids we might have had. Meanwhile, he was screwing someone else."

Emmett set the food and wine aside, wrapping his arm around her body. "I can see how you'd want to understand him and how he could do that."

"Truth be told, it went a little beyond that."

"You don't have to explain yourself to me." He tilted her chin. "You went through a dark time. You're aware of how you could have allowed yourself to be dragged into a black hole with this." He ran his thumb across her cheek. "To be honest, I'm not going to be able to rest until I've put whoever killed those men and set up your father behind bars. The only difference between you and me right now is that I get paid to have an obsession."

"While that's the sweetest thing anyone has ever said to me, you're taking a lot of time off right now to do this."

He laughed. "Yes, and no. Some of what I'm doing might be off the books, but my boss knows what I'm doing, and she's on board."

Trinity pressed her body against his and gave his lips a big kiss. It started as nothing more than a sweet thank you for being kind, but it quickly turned into something more. She clutched the fabric of his shirt, clinging so tightly that he wondered if she might rip it in half.

She pushed him to his back and straddled his legs. Her desperation matched her passion, and he became drunk on it. This was not what he had planned for the evening. Far from it. If anything, he'd thought he might sit with her, hold her for a little bit—maybe even all night. But making love hadn't even been on his mind.

Not for tonight.

"Trinity," he managed with a raspy breath. "We don't—"

"You kind of owe me."

He chuckled. "That I do," he said, holding her hips for support. "But it doesn't have to be right now. You've had a long, emotional day."

"It wasn't that long since I spent half of it sleeping or hungover."

He reached up and brushed some of her long, thick hair behind her shoulders. He stared into her adoring eyes. "I could never say no to you."

"Ha. You did last night."

He groaned. "That's a mistake I'll never make again where you're concerned." In the short time he'd known Trinity, he'd grown to care about her. Only a few women had been able to affect his heart so deeply.

Both of them had done so in a matter of weeks.

Trinity had done it in days.

If he could give her the moon and the stars, he would.

He tugged at the hem of her shirt, lifting it over her head. Reaching around her back, he unhooked her bra, letting the straps fall gently off her shoulders.

She took her hair and twirled it around some scrunchy thing on top of her head.

"Nope." He released it, allowing the strands to cascade over her body. "I like your hair."

"It gets in the way."

"I think we'll manage." His gaze shifted from her eyes to her breasts. He couldn't help it. They were both spectacular. Breathtaking, actually. "You can always put it back up if it's making either of us crazy."

"I know how to make you go nuts." She skimmed down his legs, lifting his shirt, kissing his stomach.

He thought about protesting but thought better of it. If this was what she wanted, who was he to argue? As a matter of fact, he'd give her a hand and help by getting out of his clothes.

Resting her head on his hand, he closed his eyes and did his best to relax while enjoying every sensation her hands, lips, and mouth brought to his body. She teased him while bringing him the kind of pleasure he fantasized about. She knew exactly what he wanted. How he wanted it. The pressure was precise. Every lick, squeeze, taste, and stroke were total perfection. He didn't need to guide or give direction.

All he had to do was enjoy.

And, of course, stop her before things went too far.

"Hey, you," he managed with a throaty whisper. "Up here." He tugged gently at her hair. "Time to change it up." He sucked in a deep breath, calming things down a bit. He certainly needed a few moments to collect himself. "My turn."

"You had your fun last night."

"No, I didn't." He lifted her with ease and flipped her onto her back. He suckled one breast and then the other.

She cupped his head, moaning. "That's not fair."

"Of course, it is, and you love it." He eased his hand between her legs.

"Oh, God." She arched her back and rolled her hips, matching his movements.

He didn't want to bring her over the edge. He wanted to savor that for when he was inside her. But teasing her now brought him ridiculous pleasure. He loved how her body moved with his and how she responded to his touch.

"Yes." She moaned. "Please," she begged.

His muscles tightened. The blood racing through his veins burned. He nestled himself between her legs.

She dug her nails into his shoulders and her heels into the backs of his thighs.

He did everything he could to keep things under control, but he wasn't sure that would last for very long. Her body demanded every piece of him, and he was inclined to give it to her exactly the way she wanted it. If she asked him to stand on his head, he'd do it. He didn't care. Whatever made her happy, made him ecstatic.

Her climax came on hard and fast. It engulfed him, taking him to places he'd only been able to imagine. His head spun. He held onto her, hoping he could control his release, but it proved impossible. He found her mouth and kissed her as hard as he could while his body shuddered and his mind spun.

He'd never get this woman out from under his skin.

And he didn't think he wanted to.

He ran his fingers up and down her spine as he caught his breath. He kissed the soft spot under her earlobe, feeling the sharp rise and fall of her chest as she took air into her lungs.

"Now I'm hungry," she said. "And thirsty."

He laughed. "Lucky for you, we still have a few quarter sandwiches, and I believe the kitchen might still be open."

"Oh. I could go for some of those dessert cookies."

"I'll call room service." Emmett rolled to the side, pulling the covers over their bodies. "Do we need more wine?"

"No. Just the cookies. I had enough last night. Though I won't deprive you."

"No, I'm good," he said. "Can I ask you a serious question?"

"Of course."

"Is it okay with you if I stay the night?"

"Oh, my. Aren't you the sweetest?" She wrapped her arms around him and kissed his chest. "Yes. I'm good with that. But aren't you worried about what people will think?"

"Not in the slightest." He kissed her forehead. "I'll get us some cookies and put in an order for breakfast because we're going to need it."

"Oh. Are you suggesting we might need some energy because there will be a second round?"

"It's not a suggestion."

13

Trinity hadn't blushed since she was a teenager, yet her cheeks heated. She figured they had to be bright red at this point.

Emmett reached across the table and snagged the syrup. He poured an aggressive amount over his second helping of French toast and then drizzled some onto his bacon. "You're being awfully quiet this morning."

"I feel like everyone is staring at us."

He had the nerve to chuckle. "Just Melinda and her staff, and only because I haven't spent the night here since she and I broke up. I think they find it weird and awkward."

She pushed a couple of pieces of pineapple across

her plate. "Not to mention you're on like your third breakfast. Do you always eat this much?"

"I worked up an appetite." He winked.

The corners of her mouth tipped upward in an unwanted smile. But she couldn't help it. Last night had been less about sex and more about connection. It had been a long time since she'd felt this close to another person. Trust didn't come easily to her—not after Alex. Yet she found herself letting Emmett into her heart and soul with ease.

"Keep smiling at me like that, and I'll pick you right up out of that chair and take you back to bed."

"Promises, promises," she whispered. She'd missed this part of being in a relationship. She'd avoided getting involved too deeply with anyone, never allowing anyone to get to know the real Trinity. No one saw her vulnerabilities.

However, she'd shown Emmett all of them. He'd seen deep inside her soul and hadn't left.

"Good morning, or should I say almost afternoon," Melinda said. "I see you're taking advantage of being a special guest and having breakfast for lunch, even though we stopped serving breakfast over an hour ago and don't serve lunch for another half hour."

"Sorry," Emmett said. "Your staff offered. I accepted."

"I've got a dumb question." Trinity waved her fork. "How can you call this a bed and breakfast when you serve your guests lunch? And you offer dinner when requested twenty-four hours in advance."

"First, that dinner is an up-charge, so it's not like it's part of the price of admission." Melinda placed her hand on her hip and smiled. "Second, I want to be known as the best in South Florida. I charge a little more, but I have a lot more to offer than your average B and B, though I'm not a hotel."

"Didn't I hear you're going to be on some television show about unique places to stay?" Emmett asked.

"I am. As soon as Chad gets back from his business trip, the camera crew is coming to set up and film. I didn't want to do it without my husband at my side. Speaking of his return," Melinda said, keeping her gaze focused on Trinity. "I believe you lost our bet."

Trinity swallowed. Her cheeks went from hot to on fire. "I don't think it was actually a bet."

"Oh. It was. I remember exactly, and now one of you owes me full price for your stay."

"I'm a little in the dark here." Emmett set his fork down. "What are we discussing?"

Trinity blinked. "Nothing," she said quietly.

Melinda laughed. "I bet Trinity that the two of you would end up in bed together before Chad came home. The only thing I didn't expect was that it would happen under my roof." She shifted her stance and her gaze. "The staff is seriously shocked. It's all they can talk about."

Trinity groaned. "Wonderful. That's the last thing I need."

"Relax. They love you and think you're great for Emmett," Melinda said. "Though they worry he's not good enough for you."

"Aren't you funny?" Emmett said, waving his cell. "It's Rhett. I'd better take it." He excused himself from the table.

Melinda plopped down into the empty chair and picked up one of the syrup-doused pieces of bacon. She stared at it for a long moment before scrunching her nose, tossing it back onto the plate, and shoving all of it aside.

"What's wrong?" Trinity asked.

"I can't wait for Chad to come home," Melinda said. "While I'm not a huge fan of him traveling all the time, I've gotten used to it. Besides, this place is a lot to deal with, and Chad sometimes has too many opinions." Melinda rested her elbow on the table. "I'm a bit of a control freak and have never liked being told how to do something. It used to cause problems with Emmett and me, and it causes the same problems with Chad. I'm working on it."

"Not to be rude, but you also talk around what's going on."

Melinda waved her finger. "You're quite observant."

"Now you're avoiding."

"I am." Melinda scooted closer. "I couldn't wait another second and took the test this morning. Now I'm freaking out. Chad won't be home for another day, and I can't tell him over the phone or in a text."

It took Trinity all of three seconds to figure out what Melinda was talking about, and her heart swelled with happiness for her new friend. "Are you serious? Are you sure?"

"I took it twice."

Trinity jumped out of her chair and grabbed Melinda. "I'm so excited for you."

"Of all the people I could have told…" Melinda's words trailed off as she sniffled. "That was so insensitive of me. I don't know what I was thinking."

"Stop that," Trinity said. "I'm sure you don't want

to tell others before you tell Chad, so I'm glad you felt like I was a safe place to land."

Melinda pulled back and brushed her hair from her face. "I'm bursting at the seams with happiness, but I'm terrified at the same time."

Trinity took Melinda's hands. "I can only imagine all the emotions going through your heart right now. The only advice I have for you is to relax and think only good things. Enjoy this time and try not to stress. I know it won't be easy, but you need to be as stress-free as possible."

"The stress happens in my mind. I'm even afraid to tell Chad because what if it doesn't take?"

"That's a reasonable fear," Trinity said. "A lot of women feel that way. You're not alone. Many people don't tell family and friends until they're past the third month. And I think that might be a good thing for you and Chad. But I don't want you to focus on the reason you're keeping your happiness to yourselves. Focus on being a couple and experiencing this together."

Melinda tilted her head. "Can I keep you? Forever?"

Trinity squeezed her hands. "Yes." For some reason, that brought up a flashing image of Kathy, but not in a good way.

On the outside, it appeared that Kathy was a supportive friend. She almost always answered the phone when she called. Was always willing to meet Trinity for a bite or a drink when she was having a bad day.

But while that was all good, Kathy didn't think Trinity should be defending her father. And while Kathy never once said that she thought Trinity's dad had killed those men, she'd implied it a few times. Whenever Trinity called her out on it, Kathy would hold her hands up and act all hurt and say something like, *I was only repeating what the world is saying about him. I didn't mean to make it out like I believed it.*

But maybe she did.

Hell, most people did.

"You're a good person," Melinda said. "I hope we can remain friends."

"So do I." Trinity kissed Melinda's cheek.

Melinda glanced over her shoulder as she wiped the tears that had dripped from her eyes. "I knew you and Emmett would hook up."

"It's all your fault. You put the thought in my head."

"I did nothing of the sort." Melinda laughed. "It was already there."

"That's a fair statement." Trinity watched Emmett

as he paced behind the sofa in the living room. She could tell he looked stressed about something, but she wasn't sure what. "He's really sweet, but I think I'm in over my head."

"Why?"

"It's too much, too soon."

"Honey, don't overanalyze this. Just enjoy it," Melinda said.

"And what happens when I go back to Pensacola?"

"It's not like that's the other side of the country."

There were so many reasons Trinity didn't want to get involved in a long-distance relationship. But the only one that mattered was the last time she had ended up moving to another city because she couldn't stand having every waking moment consumed by thoughts of what her boyfriend was doing.

It was so bad that she hadn't seen the signs that Alex wasn't the most tuned-in person and that he was more interested in himself and his image than her or their future together.

"I'm not good at long distance," she admitted. "The last time I did it, I gave up and moved to be with Alex."

"Oh. I see," Melinda said. "Well, Emmett is no Alex, that's for damn sure. But it's too soon to be talking about moving. Relax. Enjoy each other. See where it takes you."

The only problem was that she believed it was a dead-end road for Emmett and her.

"Here he comes, and he doesn't look too happy." Trinity stood. "What's wrong?"

"Rhett's coming back to Florida," Emmett said. "And he's bringing Shawn with him."

"Why?" Trinity asked. "Don't we think Shawn might have had something to do with all of this?"

"We did. But we have some new information, and it's leading us back to Shawn's sister, Rayna." Emmett tapped his phone. "Shawn said she's batshit crazy, and he's constantly having to bail her out of one financial mess after the other. However, they haven't spoken to or seen each other in a couple of years. Last he heard, she was living in Miami with some rich land developer. We still have very little on her, but we do have a picture." He held up his cell.

Trinity's heart dove right into the depths of Hell. She snagged the electronic device. "I don't believe it. It can't be. No fucking way."

"Do you know her?" Emmett asked.

"Yeah. She teaches yoga at the gym I belong to." Trinity blinked, hoping the image would somehow change, but it didn't. "That's my friend, Kathy."

14

"Has Kathy called or texted?" Emmett asked as he strolled across the pool patio at his mother's home. He found it interesting that Kathy had been up Trinity's ass since she'd left Pensacola, but not so much over the last twenty-four hours.

"Not since she asked me how I was doing first thing this morning. Do you want me to reach out?" Trinity asked.

"Not yet. I want to wait for Rhett."

"What about my mom and dad. I'm so worried about them."

"Don't be. They're fine. I've been able to secure a bodyguard for them." Emmett curled his fingers around Trinity's forearms.

She shrugged him off. "I can't believe Kathy is really Paul's daughter, Rayna. And that she's been lying to me, pretending to be my friend the entire time I've known her, when all she wanted was—hell, I don't know *what* she wants."

"I'm guessing she learned you had hired a private investigator to find your dad and wanted to keep tabs on what you knew. Or didn't know," Emmett said. "She needed to control the narrative and keep you from finding out the truth."

I told her everything we were doing, with the exception of the fact that we have the contents of that envelope." Trinity turned toward the ocean and pulled her wrap across her body. Her hair whipped over her shoulder in the strong breeze.

Emmett and his mother had both agreed that her house out on the island with its state-of-the-art surveillance equipment would be the safest place for not just Trinity but also the community.

He leaned against the post by the trail heading to the beach. The sun's rays danced across the water. Ever since his mother had moved into Steve's house, this had become Emmett's place to relax and reset when work got to be too much. It was somewhere he could recharge his batteries. Clear his mind.

Sometimes he came here just to think and

ponder where he wanted to go in life since it had taken a big left turn.

For now, he hoped it would be a haven for Trinity and a place he could keep her safe.

"That's good." He wrapped his arm around her waist. "Because of that, we have an advantage. Once Rhett gets here with Shawn, we can devise a plan for how to move forward."

"Can we trust Shawn? I mean, he could be in on this with his sister."

"That was my first thought, too," Emmett said. "But I trust Rhett with my life. If he thinks Shawn is telling us the truth, then so do I."

Trinity pulled away, inching closer to the path that led to the beach. She lifted her chin toward the sun. "I can't trust my judgment anymore."

He jumped out in front of her, taking a good scan of the sand. Rhett had called in a couple of private eye buddies, and they were currently strolling the beach. However, if there were a breach in security, it would be at this point. He held her by her biceps. "What are you talking about?" He stared deep into her eyes. "You knew all along that your father couldn't have killed those men. You believed in the truth and never wavered."

"But I didn't figure out that Kathy was really

Rayna. I trusted the wrong person and helped her frame my father."

"You haven't done that." He kissed her nose.

She glared. "I let her in and told her all my thoughts on my dad. All my deep feelings. I shared things with her that I didn't tell anyone else."

"I'm no psychologist, but I bet she's a master manipulator. Maybe even a psychopath."

"You're not making me feel better."

He tucked a few stray strands of hair that blew across her face behind her ear. "Let's not focus on that. The pieces of the puzzle are coming together, and we're going to clear your father's name." Emmett was more than confident that he would be able to do that in the coming days. What he wasn't sure of was how he could say goodbye to Trinity. "Lucy Ann's dad has sent more information over on Bugsy. And Cotania has been incredibly helpful in our investigation. He's given us proof that the first few murders were someone else and even got permission to re-open those cases."

She narrowed her eyes. "I didn't know that. It wasn't on the news, and we know I'm getting alerts because even Melinda thinks I'm becoming a little obsessed."

"No. I'd be doing that—take that back, I *am*

checking the news outlets on a regular basis," Emmett said. "However, because of what's going on with Robash and this case, we're all in agreement that information can't get out until we wrap this up."

She sucked in a long, slow breath and then blew it out in a big puff. "When all of this is over, I'm going to need a vacation."

Timing was everything, and this was about as piss-poor a time to do this as he could imagine. But she'd given him the perfect opening. "I have a couple of weeks off coming up. I was thinking since we didn't get to go for our boat ride, maybe we could rent a charter and go to the Bahamas for a bit. Get to know each other better. See if we want to make a go of a long-distance dating thing."

Her long lashes fluttered over her sweet eyes. "That's unexpected."

"I'm sorry. We can talk about it later." He gave her biceps a good squeeze and turned toward the house.

"No." She grabbed his shoulder. "You brought it up, and it's obvious that we like each other, but I want you to understand a few things about me."

"That would be the point of taking a trip together and then seeing how we feel when you go back to Pensacola, and I stay here." He took her mouth in a hot, passionate kiss. It was the kind that excited the body, warmed the heart, and eased the soul. He wanted to show her that he cared enough for her to risk it all. That he could put it all on the line to see where it might lead.

"Wow," she whispered. "You certainly know how to kiss."

"It's all about the lips on the other end."

She patted the center of his chest. "Here's the thing. The last long-distance relationship I got into was with Alex."

"Please don't compare me to your ex. I won't ever do that to you."

"This isn't about him," she said. "I moved to be with him too quickly because I had become consumed by him before I really got to know him. Looking back, there were signs at how unconnected to me he was. Things like him rarely coming to see me. I always had to go to Atlanta."

"I like Pensacola. I'll come visit you first."

She smiled. "You're sweet."

"I have no idea where this is heading, but I want to find out," he said. "What do you say? Want to take a trip to the Bahamas with me?"

She kissed him.

Hard.

"I take it that's a yes," he whispered.

"Hell, yes."

Movement around the side of the house caught his attention. "Rhett's here. Why don't we sit down by the pool? I don't like being this close to the beach. It would be too easy for someone to breach the perimeter. With that said, if I have to go anywhere, please stay in the house, okay?"

"If you're going somewhere, so am I."

"Not if I'm taking someone down." He rested his hand on the small of her back. "I'm not taking the chance of you getting hurt."

"I want to be there to look her in the eyes when you arrest her," Trinity said, her voice thick with emotion. "I want to tell her that I hope she rots in Hell."

"Save that speech for the courtroom, and then tone it down," Emmett said. "But I'm more concerned about the hired hitman. If Kathy was willing to have all those men murdered, she wouldn't have any problem putting a hit out on you."

Trinity stood next to Emmett and dug her fingernails into his hand. Her heart beat so fast it hurt her chest.

"Hey," Rhett said. "This is Shawn Lewis."

A tall man, who looked a lot like the old pictures Trinity remembered of Paul, stood before her. He wore jeans and a designer button-down shirt. His shoes looked as if they were Italian leather, but she couldn't be sure.

"This is my brother, Emmett, and of course, this is Trinity Hughes," Rhett continued.

"I'm sorry about what happened to your father," Shawn said. "I want you to know that I will do whatever it takes to help find my sister and whoever else she's pulled into her crazy scheme."

"Why don't we all sit down?" Emmett pulled out a chair.

Trinity flattened her hands on the table and lowered herself onto the cushion. She took in a deep, calming breath, using one of the techniques she'd learned in yoga—shit. All that did was remind her of Kathy—or Rayna. "Do we know where she is?"

"I have a buddy of mine looking for her in Pensacola, but so far nothing," Rhett said.

"I'm told she's going by the name Kathy?" Shawn asked.

Trinity nodded. "She's a yoga teacher at the gym I belong to. She and I became friends about a year ago."

"Kathy was our grandmother's name," Shawn said. "I'm not surprised she used it. When our grandma passed a couple of years ago, Rayna got worse."

"What do you mean by worse?" Trinity leaned forward and folded her hands on the table.

"My sister, and we can call her Kathy since that's how you know her, has had a lot of issues during her life. When she was younger, she saw a therapist who told us that she had a personality disorder. He put her on medication, which she never stays on. Never." Shawn shook his head. "I don't know what to do with her. I've tried cutting her off a couple of times, but she ended up in the psychiatric ward because she tried to hurt herself. Only I think she faked it to get my attention. But what an asshole I am for thinking that, right?" Shawn leaned back and blew out a puff of air. "I knew she was living in South Florida with some rich, older guy, but I haven't seen her in a couple of years."

"You must have known about the Adultery Killer and the connection to your father and to the man who killed him," Emmett said. "Did you ever think your sister could have been involved?"

"Honestly, no. But I didn't think my sister was up to any good either. She has issues, but she wasn't violent. She acted out sexually, and she's a pathological liar," Shawn said.

"What made you believe my brother so quickly?" Emmett asked.

"Kathy called me a few weeks ago asking for money." Shawn ran a hand across the top of his buzzed head. "I wasn't surprised because, every couple of years, she runs out of whatever I've given her, or whatever whomever she's been living off does after they smarten up. I told her no and hung up. Normally, she waits a week and comes back at me. But this time, she called me back in seconds. She told me she was in trouble. That her credit cards were maxed out, and she didn't have a dime. That if I didn't give her money, she would end up on the streets. I thought that was dramatic. I asked her to give me some banking information and said I'd wire her some money. The bank was in Pensacola." Shawn held up his hand. "I still hadn't thought anything of it. I also planned to make her wait a couple more days. So, when she didn't get it in a timely manner, someone claiming to be her boyfriend paid me a visit."

"That was two days ago." Rhett pulled out the picture Trinity's father had sketched of the man who'd been following him. Bugsy. Rhett tapped his finger on the picture. "Bugsy told Shawn that he and his family would end up in the Hudson River if he didn't pay."

"So, I paid. That guy was fucking scary," Shawn said.

Trinity's heart dropped to her gut. "Why didn't you call the police?"

"I've been dealing with my sister and her brand of crazy for years. While I was frightened by that man, my sister has never tried to hurt me. I had no reason to believe that this was anything but her being her usual dramatic self," Shawn said. "It wasn't until Rhett showed up that I started to believe that my sister could be behind the murders."

Emmett laced his fingers with Trinity's. "We have the upper hand now. She doesn't know we've talked to Shawn, and she doesn't know we have the contents of the envelope."

"Or that we have a sample of Bugsy's handwriting," Rhett said with a smile. "The note we got from Tony, and the signature from the bank needed for the wire transfer. We sent both to Lucy Ann's father, and he's already had it analyzed by an expert. It's a match to the notes left by the Adultery Killer."

"That's our fucking smoking gun." Emmett pounded the table. "Now we just have to find them."

"They could be halfway to Mexico by now," Trinity said as all the air in her lungs flew out. "They aren't going to want to get caught and if they think that's possible, I bet they have new identities and are long gone."

"I told you that my sister got worse after our grandma died. Part of that was because our grandmother had dementia. In the end, she had become obsessed with how her son had been killed. Minutes before she passed, she begged my sister to make sure she took care of whoever had taken her boy from her. I never thought my sister would actually do it." Shawn rubbed his chin as he let out a long breath.

Trinity could see the pain in his eyes. While her anguish was different, she could still relate. He'd lost his father when he'd been a baby. Then his mother.

And, eventually, his sister.

His life had been hard.

Perhaps harder than Trinity's.

She reached out and touched his hand. "You're not responsible for what she did."

"Aren't I, though?" A tear rolled down his cheek. "If I hadn't been bankrolling her all these years, she wouldn't have been able to hire someone to kill innocent men and frame your father for it."

"We can't dwell on these things," Emmett said. "Right now, we need to draw Kathy and Bugsy out."

"There's only one way to do that," Rhett said.

"How?" Trinity asked.

"Nope." Emmett shook his head. "No fucking way."

"What?" Trinity glanced between the two brothers. "If it will get them out in the open so you can arrest them, why aren't we doing it?"

"Because it means using you as bait," Emmett said. "I won't allow it."

Trinity swallowed the thick lump in her throat as she pulled her cell from her back pocket. "I'm not going to live in fear. And the longer she's out there, the longer I have to look over my shoulder, and the longer my father's name is trampled through the mud." She caught Emmett's gaze. "Tell me what to say and how to say it. Let's end this now."

15

Emmett paced in his mother's living room. He placed his hand on the butt of his weapon, hoping that would calm his nerves, but it didn't. If anything, it increased his pulse.

He glanced at Trinity, who sat in the extra-large accent chair by the picture window. She had her feet tucked up under her butt and held her phone in her hand as if it were a prize piece of jewelry. It wouldn't be the first time he'd used a witness or a victim to bait a suspect.

Or someone he cared about.

He'd done that with Melinda. It had all worked out fine, but it could have gone seriously sideways.

"Would you stop that?" his mother said. "You're making me nuts."

"You're making all of us nuts." Rhett leaned against one of the big pillars that connected the kitchen to the great room. "It's not going to make Kathy text back any quicker."

"When was the last time you talked with her?" Shawn asked from his perch on the sofa. "She's a game player, especially if she's on to you."

"She texted me this morning, asking how I was doing and what was going on with my search. I told her I was fine and not much." Trinity held up her phone and waved it in the air. "I'm shocked she hasn't responded to this last message. I mean, I told her that we had a lead and gave her Bugsy's name."

"She's either on a plane to a foreign country," Rhett said, "or she's planning her move and doesn't want to respond until she knows what that is."

Emmett inched closer to Trinity. "How are you holding up?"

"My heart is racing. I have chest pain, and my stomach hurts."

"Sounds about right." He took the cell.

"What the hell are you doing?" She jumped to her feet.

"It's not healthy for you to keep staring at it," Emmett said.

"I don't care. It gives me something to focus on."

The phone vibrated in his hands. He glanced down. "She texted." He cleared his throat. "It reads: *Call me when you're alone. I have information. I can't believe you were right. But you were.*"

"You know your sister," Rhett said to Shawn. "What kind of game is she playing?"

"My best guess is she wants to find out what Trinity really knows." He leaned forward. "And if you've figured out she's behind the murders. But, honestly, this goes beyond anything she's ever done before, so I feel like I'm grasping at straws."

"That's a fair assessment," Emmett said. "Okay. Let's get this party started. Put it on speaker and call her. Remember to stick as close to the truth as you can, and I'll write things down on a piece of paper to help you."

Trinity nodded.

Emmett hit the green button and handed her the phone. She sucked in a breath and sat back down.

The phone rang once.

"I'm glad you called so quickly," Kathy said. "First, are you okay? And are you alone?"

"Yes. On both accounts."

"I can't believe I didn't listen to you. I'm so sorry," Kathy said. "It's crazy to me that this Bugsy guy set your dad up, but what's even crazier is what I found out."

Emmett could only imagine what insanity this woman would come up with.

"What do you mean what you found out?" Trinity asked.

Emmett sat on the edge of the chair with a pen and a piece of paper in his hands. He stared at Trinity, who had wide eyes as she twisted a piece of hair nervously between her fingers. He squeezed her thigh in hopes of reassuring her that everything would be okay.

"I have a cousin who works cyber security for the military. I asked him to do me a favor when you told me about Bugsy. I hate to be the one to tell you this, but you need to get out of there."

"Why?"

Emmett had a bad feeling about where this was going. He scribbled on the paper.

Play along, whatever it is.

Trinity nodded.

"My cousin learned that Bugsy is friends with Emmett, the police officer that is pretending to help you. He's in on it. You're not safe."

Trinity gasped. "How can you be sure?"

"I have pictures of them. I'll text you. Just make

sure he doesn't see them. I'm worried about your safety."

"Hang on. It came through." Trinity swiped the screen, and an image of Emmett with Bugsy on a fishing trip appeared.

Emmett scribbled on the paper.

That's fake.

"I can't just up and leave. That would look suspicious."

"I'm three hours away. Give me the address of where you're staying. We can say we're going out to get a bite to eat and just leave. We'll drive down to Fort Lauderdale, meet with that FBI agent, and tell her what we know," Kathy said. "I'm so sorry I didn't believe you."

Emmett was amazed at how composed Trinity remained throughout the conversation. He wrote more notes on the paper as Rhett motioned for them to keep the call going.

Tell her it's okay. Ask her what else her cousin found out about me. How dangerous am I?

"It's okay, Kath. Even my parents thought I was nuts," Trinity said. "What else did you find out about Emmett? Because he seems so nice. So genuine. I thought he was on my side."

"I'm sure he wanted you to believe that. But he's on the take somehow. My cousin hasn't put it all together yet, but he's sure Emmett is not concerned about helping you clear your father's name. If anything, he's the reason your father was shot that day."

Emmett wanted to reach through the phone and strangle Kathy.

"I have to stop and get gas. Text me your location, and I'll see you soon."

The phone went dead.

"Not enough time," Rhett said. "We might be able to ping a hundred-mile radius, but she didn't stay on long enough for my software to work."

"She knew we were listening," Emmett said. "She had to, and I'll bet she's not three hours away. I'm sure she's in town somewhere looking for us."

"I have to agree," Rhett said. "Text her this address."

"Are you sure you want her coming to your mother's house?" Trinity asked.

"I'm not having her go anywhere else," Rhett said. "We can control the situation here."

Shawn stood. "My sister sounds on edge. Worse than I've ever heard her before. And I don't understand what she thinks she's going to get away with. If she comes back, she has to know you're on to her. That you plan on arresting her and Bugsy."

"That's just it. She thinks because she has Robash in her pocket, she's safe," Emmett said. "But she doesn't know that Cotania is in Fort Lauderdale right now on the pretext of having a meeting with Robash about something else. In reality, she's being questioned about her role in all of this. She's going down. We've got all the evidence, and we turned it over."

"It's all about timing," Rhett said.

"Give me your phone so I can send the text." Emmett held out his hand.

Trinity handed it over.

Trinity: *Here is the address of where I'm staying. When does the GPS say you'll be here?*

Kathy: *Two hours and twenty-five minutes. See you soon.*

Emmett inhaled sharply. "Let's make sure this goes down without any casualties."

Trinity stared out the front window. Five cars had driven by in the last twenty minutes, but not one had been Kathy.

She was fifteen minutes late.

Another vehicle slowed in front of the driveway before turning in.

"She's here." Trinity rubbed her hands on her thighs to keep them from shaking. But it didn't help. Every muscle vibrated from the inside out. Working in the ER, she was used to her adrenaline going from zero to sixty and then back to zero in minutes.

This was nothing like that.

"Do you think she's alone?" Trinity asked Emmett, who wrapped his arm around her waist.

"It appears she is," he said. "Rhett is on the roof. My mom is on the north end of the property, while my brother, Nathan, is at the south end. Emmerson is in the back. Cotania sent a SWAT team to the neighbor's. Robash rolled over, so we've got her. But we need to find out where Bugsy is. He's dangerous."

Trinity nodded.

"Are you ready?"

"Yes," she said with a long breath.

He kissed her cheek. "I'll be in the next room and will make my appearance when appropriate. You'll be fine."

"Easy for you to say." She shook out her arms and stood in the foyer by herself while Emmett ducked into the den.

She waited for what seemed like an eternity for the front bell to ring. Closing her eyes for a few moments, she did her best to calm her nerves and channel her inner actress.

Pulling open the door, she plastered a smile on her face. "Oh, my God. I'm so glad you're here." Trinity yanked Kathy in for a big hug, kicking the category-five door so it slammed shut.

Emmett had told her that she needed to make sure Kathy came inside the house and that she closed the door. She tried to make sure she did it in a genuine fashion.

"This isn't the bed and breakfast you were staying at," Kathy said with a hint of annoyance.

"No. It's actually Emmett's mother's house. Emmett moved me from the other place when he"—she held up her hands and made air quotes—"found out that Bugsy was the killer."

"Where is Emmett?" Kathy asked.

"He had an errand to run, but I'm sure you saw the cop car down the street. He's got someone watching me all the time."

"Well, we've got a bigger problem." Kathy looked around nervously. "Is anyone here?"

"A couple members of his mother's and her fiancé's staff, but no one else."

Kathy stepped into the great room. Quickly, she peeked down the hallway. "It turns out that FBI agent, the one I wanted us to go see? She's in on it with Emmett."

"No way." Trinity did her best to make her eyes go wide and look as shocked as possible. "How did you find that out?"

"I thought I'd better call her, but I was redirected to another agent, who informed me. It's not safe for you to go there right now. I don't know who we can trust, but my cousin hooked us up with some of his friends. They will know what to do."

If Trinity didn't know better, she'd have to question the lie. What FBI agent would tell a random citizen that another agent was on the take? That made no sense. Did Kathy really think that Trinity was that foolish? "I need to go get my things," Trinity said.

"We don't have time for that. My cousin is waiting for us."

"Where are we meeting him?"

"A few hours from here." Kathy turned and curled her fingers around the door handle. "We should really get going."

"Let me get my purse and cell."

"Leave the phone. Emmett could be tracking that."

"You know what I don't understand?" Trinity said. "Why would Emmett do this? He didn't know me. My dad. My family. It doesn't make sense to me."

"I don't know. Maybe he wanted to make a name for himself. Maybe he wanted to be the one to catch the killer, so he hired someone to do it." Kathy took Trinity by the hand. "Come on. Let's go."

Emmett had warned her that Kathy would want her to leave right away, and the point was to keep her talking for as long as she could.

"Why didn't your cousin or his friends come with you? Isn't he concerned about your safety with Bugsy still out there?"

"He's been busy doing other things so we can make sure you're no longer in danger." Kathy grabbed her by the arm, then raced back to the front door and yanked it open. "Stop asking so many questions and get moving," she snapped.

"I'm sorry, Kathy. I'm scared and confused, and I don't understand why your cousin would send you here alone if he's concerned that Emmett is so dangerous."

"I don't have time for this," Kathy mumbled as

she opened her bag and pulled out a gun. She pointed it at Trinity. "Let's go."

Trinity gasped and took a step back. "What the hell are you doing? Why do you have a weapon, Kathy?" She clutched her chest. She could feel her heart pounding.

"Put the gun down." Emmett's voice bellowed from somewhere behind her. It calmed her for a brief second.

"You stupid bitch." Kathy pointed the gun right in Trinity's face. "Now, I'm going to have to have Bugsy kill some innocent people. Like his ex, Melinda." She jerked the gun at Emmett.

"That's not going to happen," Emmett said with a confident tone.

Kathy wrapped her free hand around Trinity's arm, pulling her close as she shoved the gun against her side.

Trinity groaned, and tears welled in her eyes. She couldn't let anything happen to Melinda and her unborn child. "I'll go with you if you promise not to hurt Melinda."

"Oh. Is she your new best friend?" Kathy asked. "Do you bond over bagels while sitting on the dock watching boats go by?"

Trinity's jaw dropped open. "You've been here this entire time. Watching me. Us."

Kathy shrugged. "You should have let this go. If you could have done that, we wouldn't be in this situation."

"You're the one with the problem." Emmett inched closer, holding his weapon high.

Kathy laughed. "The only issue I have is how to wrap all this up so it doesn't come back on me. But I'm not worried. Now, Trinity and I are going to walk out of here, and you're not going to do anything about it. If you do, Melinda is dead. And don't think that's not the case because Bugsy is with her right now, waiting for my call."

"Fuck." Emmett stood in the center of the front door and watched as Trinity climbed into the passenger seat of Kathy's car.

"Mom's five minutes from Melinda's place," Rhett's voice crackled in Emmett's ear. "Emmerson is ready to follow. Don't worry."

Easier said than done.

He tapped the earpiece. "I'm fucking freaking out. Do we have eyes on the bed and breakfast?"

"No. And Melinda isn't answering her cell."

"I don't like this."

"As soon as they pull out of the driveway, you and I can be on our way to the B&B. I have Find My Phone working with Emmerson."

Emmett knew his brother was right. If the tables were turned, he'd be saying all the same things. But it killed him that he had to watch Trinity drive away with a woman holding a loaded gun on her. That hurt his heart in ways he hadn't expected.

His chest tightened as Kathy backed the vehicle to the edge of the street. "Come on. We can't let them drive away. Talk to me."

"Mom just pulled into the bed and breakfast. Give her a chance to go check it out."

Emmett inched down the driveway. The second the car pulled out onto the road, he took off jogging. Not that he would chase them down the street, but he couldn't stand that he couldn't see Trinity anymore.

He pulled out his cell. "Add me to Mom's call."

"Sure thing," Rhett said.

It took about thirty seconds for the call to connect.

"Mom? Are you there?" Emmett asked. "What's going on?"

"Melinda's fine," his mother said. "Bugsy's sitting in a car down the street. I'm waiting for backup before I take him in."

"Let us know when he's in custody," Emmett said.

"You got it. Be safe," his mother said.

"Get Emmerson to stop Kathy before the bridge." Emmett turned and glanced up at the roof.

Rhett was already getting down.

Emmett raced toward his SUV, climbing behind the driver's seat and hitting the start button.

Rhett jumped into the passenger seat and held up his cell. "I've got Emmerson on the horn."

"Emmerson, see if you can call the bridge and ask them to raise it. I don't want to risk them getting off the island." Emmett punched the gas. By his calculations, it had been four minutes since Trinity and Kathy had pulled out of the driveway.

They could be at least a mile or two down the road.

The bridge was five miles away.

"Consider it done," Emmerson said.

"Where are you?' Rhett asked.

"I'm three miles from the house, and I can see them in my rearview," Emmerson said.

"There they are." Rhett indicated. "Let's box them in."

"We need to be careful. That bitch has a loaded gun pointed at my girlfriend."

"Oh. Is that what you're calling her now? Does Mom know?" Rhett teased.

"If Ma knew, she probably wouldn't have willingly gone to Melinda's. She would have sent one of you so she could have saved her. But, no, Trinity is mine to save."

"She's not a possession," Rhett said.

"You know what I mean."

"The bridge is going up," Rhett said. "Slow down and ease in behind them in the other lane."

"You got it."

Emmett rested his weapon on his lap as he rolled his vehicle to a stop about three car lengths behind Kathy and Trinity. "Ready?"

"I'm ready," Emmerson said.

"Let's do this."

"Why?" Trinity asked.

"Why what?" Kathy flew down the road, going at least fifteen to twenty miles over the speed limit.

"Why set my father up? Why befriend me? Why all of it?" Trinity tried not to focus on the gun that

Kathy held in her hand and kept trained on Trinity, but it proved impossible. She worried that if they hit a pothole, Kathy might accidentally pull the trigger and kill Trinity.

She swallowed that thought.

"Everyone always wants to know the why. Does it really matter?"

"It does to me," Trinity said. "I get that you feel my father wronged you."

Kathy turned her head. "So, you know who I really am."

"I do."

"And how long have you known that?"

"I just found out today," Trinity said. "But that still doesn't justify the why. You were a baby when my father killed yours. And my dad did his time. He hasn't hurt anyone since then. Why hold this grudge all these years? And why become my friend? I don't think you planned on killing me." She glanced down at the gun. "But now, I think that's changed." She shouldn't be antagonizing a woman who had a loaded weapon pointed at her rib cage. However, she had to trust that Emmett and his family were only one to two steps behind her and would make sure that Melinda was safe.

Trinity pressed her hand over her middle.

Melinda and her baby had to be safe. Trinity would never forgive herself if anything bad happened to them.

"Fucking bridges in this town," Kathy mumbled as the car slowed. "Since we're going to be stuck here for a few minutes, I'll give you a little history lesson."

"Okay." Trinity's heart lurched when she caught a glimpse of the vehicle rolling to a stop behind them.

Emmett.

She needed to keep her cool. This was going to end. She needed to make sure it ended without a bullet tearing through her body.

"My grandmother died begging me to make sure the man who took her baby boy—my father—from her went back to prison where he belonged. She believed that your dad got off too easy. She tasked me with making sure that he suffered and perhaps saw the death penalty. She also wanted his family to feel the kind of pain she did. It wasn't fair. I have to agree."

Trinity glanced in the side mirror. Neither Emmett nor Rhett were in Emmett's vehicle any longer. Her pulse sored. She had to keep her cool. Getting shot wasn't on her bucket list.

"I'm honestly very sorry about what my dad did

all those years ago, but that has nothing to do with me."

"You're right. It doesn't," Kathy said. "I never had any intention of hurting you, but you wouldn't let this go. You had to come here and poke the bear. If you had just let things go and let your father take the fall, we wouldn't be sitting here right now."

"You had innocent men killed because you wanted my father to go back to prison?"

"They weren't innocent," Kathy said. "They were cheating bastards just like my dad. Just like your mom. Just like my grandpa. They deserved to pay for their crimes. And more than the slaps on the wrists they had been given."

Before Trinity could open her mouth to say anything, both the driver's and passenger-side doors flew open.

"What the hell?" Kathy said as she lifted the gun.

"I wouldn't do that if I were you." Emmerson reached across her and knocked the weapon away. He lifted his gun, pointing it at Kathy. "You're under arrest."

"Are you okay?" Emmett lifted Trinity out of the passenger seat and into his arms. "Are you hurt?"

"No. I'm fine." She wrapped her hands around his strong frame. "Melinda? Are she and the baby safe?"

"Baby?" Emmett set Trinity's feet on the ground about twenty feet from the road.

She glanced over her shoulder.

Kathy screamed obscenities at Emmerson as he slapped the handcuffs on and Mirandized her.

"Melinda's pregnant?" Emmett asked with an arched brow.

"Shit. You can't tell anyone. Chad doesn't know yet."

"Wow. That's exciting. You're going to have to tell me when we're on our boating excursion to the Bahamas how and why she told you and not her husband first." He cupped her face. "Are you sure you're okay? I'm so sorry I had to let you leave with that lunatic."

She curled her fingers around his wrists. "I'm fine. You did what you had to do in order to save all of us."

He kissed her lips tenderly. "I care about you. I know it's crazy to say that because we barely know each other, but I have real, deep feelings for you, and I want to explore them."

Sirens blared. Red lights flashed in the sky as a couple of police cars raced to the scene.

She ignored all of that and focused on the man who made her heart beat a little faster. "I want to explore my feelings, too."

He tilted his head. "May I kiss you like I mean it right here on the side of the road in front of a couple of my brothers and a few colleagues?"

She wrapped her arms around his shoulders and leaned into his strong body. "Before any lip-lock happens, I need to thank you for saving me."

"I didn't do that," he said. "Or, at least, I didn't do that alone. I had help from my family, and from you."

When his mouth pressed against hers, she melted into his arms. She could deny and lie to herself about a lot of things, but how hard and fast she was falling for Emmett would be impossible to hide from. The only thing she could do was let it happen.

"I'm going to have a bunch of shit to do tonight," Emmett whispered. "I know Melinda is going to be freaked out. Maybe I should take you back there, and you can hang out with her while I take care of business. I'll book our vacation for a couple of days."

She stared into his warm eyes. "I need to see my parents before I do that. And make arrangements at work."

"Tell me when you want to go, and I'll make it happen." He kissed her nose. "And I'd love to meet your folks, so maybe I'll make a trip to Pensacola first."

"I'm not sure I'm ready for that." She dropped her head to his chest. "Can we wait until we see where we are after our trip?"

"Whatever you want. Just know that I'm here for you."

"Thank you." Trinity had no idea what the future held, but for the first time in a long while, she knew that her life wouldn't be consumed by the past or by anger.

16

THE BAHAMAS, THREE WEEKS LATER...

Trinity rolled over and blinked open her eyes. The sun peeked through the porthole of her and Emmett's stateroom on their charter boat. It was the last morning of their two-week vacation, and Trinity didn't want it to end.

"Good morning, beautiful." Emmett pulled her into his arms and kissed her. Hard.

Like he did every morning.

She could get used to this.

And not so much the boat and the water and luxury, though that was nice, thanks to Steve, Emmett's soon-to-be stepfather. It was more about being with Emmett.

She'd fallen in love with him, hook, line, and sinker.

Now, all she had to do was tell him how she felt and hope that he had the same deep feelings.

"I can't believe we have to go back to reality today," she said.

"I'm more bummed that you're going to Pensacola, and I'm going to Lighthouse Cove," he said. "If I had my way, we'd be going to the same town."

She palmed his cheek. "Don't you think it would be crazy for us to do something so nuts, considering we've only known each other for such a short period of time?"

"Life is too short not to take chances," he said. "I love you."

"You what?" She jerked her back and blinked.

"You heard me," he said. "Do you love me back?"

A million things raced through her mind, but the only one that mattered was the fact that this man meant more to her than anyone else, outside of her parents. "Yes. I love you."

He smiled like a big kid.

"I know you're worried about a lot of different things, and if you want me to move to Pensacola, I will. I'm sure I could get a job with the local police department there."

"You'd do that for me?"

"Not you. For us."

Tears burned her eyes. "No. You can't leave Lighthouse Cove, and I don't want you to. Your family is there."

"Your parents are in North Florida."

"They might move. They talk about it all the time," she said. "Besides, I can get a job anywhere and—"

He pressed his finger over her lips. "You did that once for a man, and it didn't work out. I want us to work out, so I'd rather do it for you."

"That is why I love you," she said, holding back a sob. "But I'm kind of attached to Lighthouse Cove now. And Melinda wants me to be godmother to her baby. There are so many other reasons for me to move."

"Sweetheart, I don't want you to do anything you will regret. I love you and want to make you happy. I can be happy anywhere, as long as I'm with you."

"I feel the same way, but I think we'll both be happier in Lighthouse Cove. It's our haven," Trinity said. "But there is one other thing I think we should talk about."

"What's that?"

"Family," she said with her heart hanging in the

wind. "I want one, and while neither of us can have one, the old—"

He pressed his finger over her lips again. "I've always wanted to adopt. And I don't need an infant. I'm good with an older child. Or two, or three."

"We just might be a perfect match," she whispered as she snuggled in closer. She couldn't imagine being with anyone who loved her and appreciated her more than Emmett did. They wanted the same things out of life, and they were both willing to do whatever it took to make their world work.

They were each other's safe harbor.

Thank you for taking the time to read *Mine to Save*.
Please feel free to leave an honest review!

Sign up for my Newsletter (https://dl.bookfunnel.com/82gm8b9k4y) where I often give away free books before publication.

Join my private Facebook group (https://www.facebook.com/groups/191706547909047/) where I post exclusive excerpts and discuss all things murder and love!

ABOUT THE AUTHOR

Jen Talty is the *USA Today* Bestselling Author of Contemporary Romance, Romantic Suspense, and Paranormal Romance. In the fall of 2020, her short story was selected and featured in a 1001 Dark Nights Anthology.

Regardless of the genre, her goal is to take you on a ride that will leave you floating under the sun with warmth in your heart. She writes stories about broken heroes and heroines who aren't necessarily looking for romance, but in the end, they find the kind of love books are written about :).

She first started writing while carting her kids to one hockey rink after the other, averaging 170 games per year between 3 kids in 2 countries and 5 states. Her first book, IN TWO WEEKS was originally published in 2007. In 2010 she helped form a publishing company (Cool Gus Publishing) with *NY Times* Bestselling Author Bob Mayer where she ran the technical side of the business through 2016.

Jen is currently enjoying the next phase of her life… the empty nester! She and her husband reside in Jupiter, Florida.

Grab a glass of vino, kick back, relax, and let the romance roll in…

Sign up for my Newsletter (https://dl.bookfunnel.com/82gm8b9k4y) where I often give away free books before publication.

Join my private Facebook group (https://www.facebook.com/groups/191706547909047/) where I post exclusive excerpts and discuss all things murder and love!

Never miss a new release. Follow me on Amazon:amazon.com/author/jentalty

And on Bookbub: bookbub.com/authors/jentalty

ALSO BY JEN TALTY

Brand new series: SAFE HARBOR!

MINE TO KEEP

MINE TO SAVE

MINE TO PROTECT

Check out LOVE IN THE ADIRONDACKS!

SHATTERED DREAMS

AN INCONVENIENT FLAME

THE WEDDING DRIVER

NY STATE TROOPER SERIES (also set in the Adirondacks!)

In Two Weeks

Dark Water

Deadly Secrets

Murder in Paradise Bay

To Protect His own

Deadly Seduction

When A Stranger Calls

His Deadly Past

The Corkscrew Killer

Brand New Novella for the First Responders series

A spin-off from the NY State Troopers series

PLAYING WITH FIRE

PRIVATE CONVERSATION

THE RIGHT GROOM

AFTER THE FIRE

CAUGHT IN THE FLAMES

CHASING THE FIRE

Legacy Series

Dark Legacy

Legacy of Lies

Secret Legacy

Emerald City

INVESTIGATE AWAY

Colorado Brotherhood Protectors

Fighting For Esme

Defending Raven

Fay's Six

Yellowstone Brotherhood Protectors

Guarding Payton

Candlewood Falls

RIVERS EDGE

THE BURIED SECRET

ITS IN HIS KISS

LIPS OF AN ANGEL

It's all in the Whiskey

JOHNNIE WALKER

GEORGIA MOON

JACK DANIELS

JIM BEAM

WHISKEY SOUR

WHISKEY COBBLER

WHISKEY SMASH

IRISH WHISKEY

The Monroes

COLOR ME YOURS

COLOR ME SMART

COLOR ME FREE

COLOR ME LUCKY

COLOR ME ICE

COLOR ME HOME

Search and Rescue

PROTECTING AINSLEY

PROTECTING CLOVER

PROTECTING OLYMPIA

PROTECTING FREEDOM

PROTECTING PRINCESS

PROTECTING MARLOWE

DELTA FORCE-NEXT GENERATION

SHIELDING JOLENE

SHIELDING AALYIAH

SHIELDING LAINE

SHIELDING TALULLAH

SHIELDING MARIBEL

The Men of Thief Lake

REKINDLED

DESTINY'S DREAM

Federal Investigators

JANE DOE'S RETURN

THE BUTTERFLY MURDERS

THE AEGIS NETWORK

The Sarich Brother

THE LIGHTHOUSE

HER LAST HOPE

THE LAST FLIGHT

THE RETURN HOME

THE MATRIARCH

More Aegis Network

MAX & MILIAN

A CHRISTMAS MIRACLE

SPINNING WHEELS

HOLIDAY'S VACATION

Special Forces Operation Alpha

BURNING DESIRE

BURNING KISS

BURNING SKIES

BURNING LIES

BURNING HEART

BURNING BED

REMEMBER ME ALWAYS

The Brotherhood Protectors

Out of the Wild

ROUGH JUSTICE

ROUGH AROUND THE EDGES

ROUGH RIDE

ROUGH EDGE

ROUGH BEAUTY

The Brotherhood Protectors

The Saving Series

SAVING LOVE

SAVING MAGNOLIA

SAVING LEATHER

Hot Hunks

Cove's Blind Date Blows Up

My Everyday Hero – Ledger

Tempting Tavor

Malachi's Mystic Assignment

Needing Neor

Holiday Romances

A CHRISTMAS GETAWAY

ALASKAN CHRISTMAS WHISPERS

CHRISTMAS IN THE SAND

Heroes & Heroines on the Field

TAKING A RISK

TEE TIME

A New Dawn

THE BLIND DATE

SPRING FLING

SUMMERS GONE

WINTER WEDDING

THE AWAKENING

The Collective Order

THE LOST SISTER

THE LOST SOLDIER

THE LOST SOUL

THE LOST CONNECTION

THE NEW ORDER